GUMSHOES: The Case of Madison's Father

Russell Nohelty

ISBN 978-1-942350-06-4
First Edition, January, 2015

For my mother, who always thought I should be a writer.

Chapter 1

Gumshoes Headquarters

Thirteen-year-old Stuart Greenbaum lay on his stomach in the grass across from Mrs. Pennybottom's house. Using his powerful binoculars, he stared past the white picket fence, watching her front door.

There was nothing Stuart loved in the world more than sleuthing. He longed to be like Dan Dash, the classic pulp comic detective with the bushy mustache and brown fedora. When Dan Dash walked into a room, he became the center of attention.

Someday, Stuart thought, that would be him. For now, he had to be content with standing in the periphery, the shadows, unnoticed by teachers and classmates alike. See, he was not particularly tall or athletic. He had no musical talent, and nobody ever wanted to cheat off his papers. Yes, by all accounts, Stuart was an average kid with a very weird hobby. But nothing would stop him from dreaming—or from wearing his Dan Dash footie pajamas while on the job.

Stuart turned on his walkie-talkie. "I'm so bored and tired. Can't crimes ever happen on my time? It's too early."

The walkie-talkie crackled to life, and a nasally, high-pitched voice responded to him. "The hen is nearing the basket."

"*Over*," Stuart said. "You're supposed to say *over*."

"Don't correct me, Stuart. I find this primitive technology well below my vast intellect. Anybody with a fourth grade education has access to a smartphone these days."

"I like it old school, just like Dan Dash."

"You and that stupid D——"

"Don't call Dan Dash stupid. He's the greatest detective of all time."

"He's a comic book character! I pity that you idolize a fictional character—especially one that uses such antiquated methods of investigation."

Wait a minute, Stuart thought, the voice is getting closer. Stuart turned from his surveillance post to see the insurmountably awkward, exceptionally geeky, thirteen-year-old Timothy Jorgenson, Stuart's business partner at the Gumshoes Detective Agency, best friend, and bane of his existence.

Timothy wore thick, Coke-bottle glasses and never combed his hair. His clothes were often stained with the residue from some botched experiment or failed compound. As a rule he preferred the gentle hum of a computer monitor to human interaction, and his love affair with science kept him indoors even on the year's most beautiful day.

"You suck the fun out of everything!" Stuart said. "Well, is there anything you'd like to say for yourself?"

"Absolutely," Timothy said. "I believe that our target is making his move."

Stuart crouched down, hiding himself behind the oak tree that had stood across from Mrs. Pennybottom's house longer than anyone could remember.

Stuart grabbed Timothy by his gangly left arm and pulled him to the ground. "You're about as subtle as a freight train."

They watched as a balding, slovenly, middle-aged man, dressed in an ill-fitting robe, snaked his way up to Mrs. Pennybottom's front porch. As he slithered up the front stoop, he craned his neck around, on the lookout for potential observers. Once satisfied that his crime would go unnoticed, he snatched up the newspaper.

"I love this part," Stuart said.

Believing he had successfully masterminded the crime of

the century, the man opened the newspaper with the slyest of grins on his face. But a blue paint bomb exploded from inside the paper, splattering all over his face and clothes.

As the man wiped the evidence off his face, doors around the block opened and guttural laughter exploded from every stoop. If he had not been covered in blue from head to toe, the man would have surely turned a vibrant shade of red.

The rumble of laughter died down, and the Pennybottom's front door opened. There stood Jill Pennybottom, chuckling under her breath. "Don't know anything about who's been stealing our paper, ay Bill?"

***

Daylight broke as Stuart and Timothy stood on the front stoop of Mrs. Pennybottom's house, watching her dole out coins one by one at an excruciatingly slow pace.

"That's two dollars and fifty cents for each of you. Thanks so much, Gumshoes. You were worth every penny. I'll be sure to tell all my friends about you guys."

The Gumshoes yawned loudly as Mrs. Pennybottom patted them on the tops of their heads. "Thanks, Mrs. Pennybottom." Stuart and Timothy turned and walked down the path away from the house, counting their pittance.

"*Penny* is the operative word," Timothy said. "Those paint bombs cost five and a quarter times more than what we charged her. We're losing our shirts."

Stuart agreed. "We're going to have to get a job to finance our job, Tim. At least we have some time before we go to school."

"I think you're mistaken," Timothy said. "While we thought the perpetrator would make his move at a quarter after five, his actual crime wasn't committed until six thirty."

Stuart panicked. "So you're saying our bus should be coming——"

"In roughly thirty seconds," Timothy said.

Stuart looked toward the end of the street and saw the bright-yellow school bus screech to a stop. He watched one of his classmates shuffle onto the bus. Then he turned and sprinted in the opposite direction.

Timothy shouted after him. "You're going in the wrong direction."

Stuart did not break stride. "Thanks, genius. I'm not ready. I'm still in my pj's."

"The bus just pulled away!"

As Timothy caught up to Stuart, the bus turned up a cul-de-sac, headed toward another group of middle schoolers.

"If you hurry up, we'll catch it before it comes back around," Stuart shouted over his shoulder.

***

Stuart stopped to catch his breath in front of a large, gnarled oak tree. The tree was the tallest in the neighborhood and grew in Timothy's yard. From the top of the tree, one got a panoramic view of the entire neighborhood—from Mr. James's ill-advised morning yoga routine to Mrs. Rigglemeyer's prize-winning begonias. Now, at the highest point of the massive oak was the largest tree house in five counties, as observed by the *East Willow Chronicle*.

The tree house, Timothy's reward for perfect report cards from ages three through ten, had taken six months to build. It had not only every modern convenience but also every possible device any able-bodied genius would need to solve crimes.

Security had been the biggest challenge to the design of the tree house. With all the costly equipment inside those walls, Timothy and Stuart wanted insurance against any unauthorized individuals who might attempt to access Gumshoes headquarters.

Timothy reached into his book bag and pulled out a little remote control. This was Timothy's ingenious solution to the security question. He pressed the button. A ladder came down, and they climbed up. He pressed the button a second time and the ladder retracted, securing the entrance to the tree house. Only two remotes existed, and they were exclusively controlled

Gumshoes: The Case of Madison's Father

by the members of the Gumshoes Detective Agency.

***

After climbing the ladder, Stuart and Timothy walked through the front door, which was emblazoned with the words "AUTHORIZED PERSONNEL ONLY!!!" For the most part, no one else really wanted to enter anyway, so there was not much need for such a stern warning. Nobody, of course, except Stuart's mother, who tried to sneak in at least once a week with snacks or some other half-baked excuse to check in on her son.

Large openings ran along the entire length of each wall and allowed the Gumshoes detectives to view any crime within a ten-block radius. Each opening was equipped with a powerful telescope. The telescopes could see even a small object—such as a hummingbird's eye—from two thousand feet away.

The room was split down the center lengthwise by a wooden counter. Each side of the room was a haven for one of the inhabitants. The left side housed a small kitchen—complete with a fully stocked stack fridge, a huge TV, an assortment of video games, and stacks of old Dan Dash comic books piled to the ceiling. This was Stuart's sanctum.

The right side of the room was the antithesis of the left. It was Timothy's domain. A row of computer monitors sat along the counter and blocked Timothy's view of Stuart's squalor.

Timothy tried, as much as possible, to create a laboratory that would be devoid of Stuart's disgusting and slovenly behavior. Unfortunately, he rarely succeeded.

***

Stuart dug through his massive clothing pile, throwing clothes skyward as he searched for anything that did not smell like rancid milk. In his frantic rush to meet the bus, Stuart threw on the first haphazard outfit he could find: an oversized shirt with a big smiley face, green shorts, a running shoe, and a dress shoe.

Timothy chuckled. "This doesn't work."

Stuart tore off his clothes and tried on another outfit. Timothy ran over to the opening that was opposite the door and began tracking the bus.

"The bus is almost here," Timothy said. "Please hurry up. We can't be tardy."

"Just give me thirty more seconds," Stuart said.

Timothy turned around to scoff at Stuart, but much to his surprise, Stuart now wore an acceptable outfit and had even run a brush through his hair. Stuart threw on his backpack. "Well, are you just going to stand there or are you going to hop to?"

"I do so hate this part," Timothy said.

"Quit being a baby." Stuart hopped onto the ledge next to

Timothy.

The zip line, which ran from the balcony to the street below, was the result of a moment of sheer brilliance, Stuart had often proclaimed. He had sold the idea as a method of quickly stopping perpetrators in their tracks; however, he only ever used it to cram in an extra three minutes of sleep before dinner.

Timothy had protested the use of the zip line since its installation and only agreed to use it in the direst of circumstances. Certainly, tardiness to school was the direst circumstance Timothy could imagine—short of receiving any grade lower than an A.

Stuart patted Timothy on the back as he pushed him up to the ledge. "Hold on tight, buddy. Don't be afraid to really wrap on."

Stuart grabbed hold of the zip line. Timothy grumbled and wrapped his arms around his friend's chest, legs, and waist so tightly that Stuart lost a little feeling in his midsection.

"You ready?" Stuart asked.

"N-o-o-o!" Timothy said.

But Stuart didn't care. He pushed off from the window, and they sped down to the street below just as the bus rounded the corner.

Stuart laughed as the breeze flowed through his hair. "See,

this isn't so bad!"

Timothy squeezed Stuart tighter. "Speak for yourself!"

They were halfway down when the school bus stopped dead in the path of the zip line. Stuart kicked his legs, trying valiantly to fight gravity and slow himself. "Oh no. Oh no. This is not good——"

Bam! They slammed right into the side of the bus. Timothy lost his grip on Stuart and fell to the ground in a heap. Stuart, stuck to the bus for a brief second, peaked into the nearest window when he heard the cacophony of laughter directed at him. His humiliation was complete when gravity pulled him down off the bus. He landed right on top of Timothy.

"That could have gone better," Stuart said.

"Agreed," Timothy said.

***

The school bus door swung open. Mrs. Haggerty sat in the driver's seat, smiling at them. Her teeth looked like they had been replaced by little flecks of baked beans, and the sight of them caused Stuart to gag every time he saw her.

"You scratched my bus, peanuts," said Mrs. Haggerty. "I love this bus more 'n my own flesh 'n blood. So imagine how much more I'm lik'n you two."

"We'll be more careful next time, Mrs. Haggerty," Stuart and Timothy said in unison. "We promise."

"Just sit down 'n shut your traps," she said.

Stuart and Timothy made their way through the bus to a chorus of chuckles and boos from every face they passed. Every time they attempted to sit down, a disapproving scowl or a threatening glare forced them to continue their shameful march. Finally, they found an open seat toward the back of the bus and slid into it, hoping to disappear from sight. Mrs. Haggerty shot daggers at them as she popped the clutch and drove away.

Their efforts at invisibility proved unsuccessful, however, as they heard the familiar, gruff voice of the monstrous figure lumbering toward them. The powerful footsteps shook the entire bus with every step. Stuart and Timothy shivered as they hoped against hope that it would pass them unnoticed.

"Hey, nerds!" The words echoed through every nook and cranny on the bus. "Nice show you two dorks put on."

"Oh no," Stuart said. "Chet."

"Maybe he'll go away," Timothy said.

But they would have no such luck. The monstrous figure stopped inches from their faces. His enormous shadow blotted out the sun. As the monstrosity sank down to address them, drool fell off its chin and splashed in a puddle at Stuart's feet. Next to Stuart, Timothy stiffened as the foul stench of Chet's breath reached him. The shadowy, red-haired mass moved into the light and fixed its beady eyes on Stuart. Chet Oliver was the worst nightmare of anybody attending East Willow Middle School and the oldest eighth grader in the history of the school by several years. It was rumored that he had been held back five times because the high school principal feared for his life in Chet's presence.

"I thought maybe, after I'd promised to pound you into the dirt, you babies would be too chicken to ride the bus today," Chet said.

Stuart puffed out his chest in an attempt to act tough but his voice cracked. "Just move on, Chet. There's nothing to see here."

"Baby got a backbone? That's a laugh! Everybody laugh!" The entire bus erupted into laughter. "I brought something for you dweebs."

Chet reached into his pocket and held up a rotten egg with his left hand. The pungent smell wafted through the entire bus. Twin girls in the front row choked back vomit, and other students desperately tried to open their windows.

"I swiped it from my mom's this morning," Chet said.

"Hmm, it seems rancid," Tim said. "Your mother should read the expiration date on her food more carefully. I'm actually quite surprised you haven't eaten it yourself by now, given your sizable girth and lack of a refined palette."

"Tim, shut it," Stuart whispered.

"Why? It's true, Stuart. He's a very large boy, or man, or boy-man, and the fact he hasn't already consumed available food is quite a testament to his will. Are you on a new diet, Chet?"

Chet fumed. "What did you say, runt?"

Stuart held his arms over his face, protecting himself from the inevitable blow that could render him unconscious until he turned eighteen. "He's going to kill us. Chet, buddy, he's just kidding. You know Tim. Such a kidder. Right, Tim?"

Chet scoffed and raised his massive left hand over his head. He slammed the egg over Stuart's head, mashing it deep into his hair follicles. The egg dripped down, covering his clothing and enveloping Stuart in its horrific stench from head to toe. "Awesome."

Chapter 2

Brilliant Deduction

Stuart stood in front of the bathroom sinks in the upstairs bathroom of East Willow Middle School, wearing nothing except his Dan Dash boxers. He had filled two of the sinks with water to soak his shirt and pants, and he vigorously lathered his hair with hand soap in the third.

"No matter what I do, it's not coming off!" Stuart said.

Timothy stood next to the door, checking his math homework on his graphing calculator. "I told you that the molecular composition of ova makes extraction without proper cleaning chemicals next to impossible. You should contact your parents, and hopefully, they can bring you a proper change of clothing."

"Well, that's all well and good, but I still have to get through the halls wearing nothing but my Skivvies. Wow, I didn't think this out, did I?"

"What about your gym clothes?" Timothy said. "I'm sure they would be an effective substitute until your mother brings you an appropriate change of clothing."

"You're a genius. Can you do me a favor?"

"Not only can I, but I will—depending on the nature of this favor. You know, on second thought, I don't like committing to a favor before hearing it. After all, you could have me swimming in pig slop or eating an earthworm."

"Quit being paranoid. All I need you to do is go to my locker and get my gym shorts. Can you do that for me, buddy?"

Timothy considered every conceivable possibility before responding. "Yes. I don't see how that could get me in trouble. I'll do it."

"Great, buddy. Combination is twenty-six, forty-seven, nine. Got it?"

Timothy nodded his head and ran out of the bathroom. As the door closed, Stuart saw three girls walking toward the door. He glanced at the sign on the door and turned pale: he was in the girls' room!

Okay, Stuart thought, stay calm. You were distracted this

morning. It's not your fault. People go into the wrong bathroom all the time. It's not weird. You'll just explain to them why you're in the wrong bathroom, wearing your underwear.

"That's ridiculous," he said. "There's no way they're not gonna think I'm a pervert."

Thinking fast, Stuart lunged for the door and locked it, just as one of the girls reached out to grab the handle.

The handle jiggled as they tried to get in. "What's going on here?"

They banged on the door, causing such a ruckus that Stuart heard the distinct clicking of Vice Principal Torres's loafers walking toward them. He slammed on the door. "This is the Vice Principal. I demand this door be opened right now!"

Well you're in it now, Stuart thought. He opened his mouth, trying to sound as mature as possible. "Sorry, but this bathroom is closed for repairs. The flooding from the flabsterlater has made everything smell like rotten eggs. We should have it fixed in about an hour or so. Don't want these kids to blow chunks in here. Really nasty business."

Stuart waited, beads of sweat forming on his brow. Silence. Then, Torres spoke. "Affirmative. I expect an update every ten minutes until the situation is resolved. Is that clear?"

"Crystal clear, sir," Stuart said. "You can count on me."

The footsteps moved away, and Stuart walked over to the

sink. He dabbed the sweat from his face with a paper towel. After several seconds of blissful silence, he nearly jumped out of his skin when he heard another slam on the door, louder this time—as if somebody had walked straight into it at full force.

"Ow!" Timothy said. "Stuart, open this door right now."

Stuart ran over to the door. "Timothy?"

"Who else would it be?" Timothy practically screamed at the door. "Now let me inside. I might have a concussion. I feel woozy."

"Quit causing a scene. You're fine." Stuart cracked open the door and peered out. The entire eighth grade class and Vice Principal Torres stood around the bathroom door, laughing their hardest. Stuart, mortified, looked down to see Timothy on the ground rubbing his head.

Timothy held up the gym shorts. "I believe you requested these."

***

Stuart and Timothy sat in Vice Principal Torres's office—the one place in East Willow Middle avoided in every possible way by every single student. After all, Torres's mean scowl and tight, military crew cut struck fear into the hearts of everybody, students and faculty alike.

"What were you two maggots thinking? The girl's bathroom? I could suspend you for this blatant act of disobedience," Vice Principal Torres screamed. "What do you have to say for yourselves? There better be a jolly good explanation."

Stuart's wet hair dripped on his unkempt gym clothes. "Well, you see sir, it's actually a funny story. This morning I was on the bus and wouldn't you know it, my breakfast fell all over my, um, entire body. When we got to school, I went to the bathroom to wash it off. But wouldn't you have it all, I must've been so frazzled I misread the sign. Come on, Mr. Torres, haven't you ever misread a sign before?"

Torres's face cracked into the mildest of smiles. "I'm going to be generous with you two pond scum because I've never had the displeasure of disciplining you before. Count your lucky stars from here to Graceland."

"Really? That is so cool of you!" Stuart said.

"Go to class, boys. I'll see you in detention for the rest of your natural-born lives."

***

Three, seventeen, twenty-one. Timothy opened his locker. "I've never had a single blemish on my record. My father will be furious."

"Can you believe that guy?" Stuart said. "Detention for the rest of our lives—that's just not fair. Doesn't he think the embarrassment is punishment enough?"

A large group of girls passed them in the hallway. They chuckled, snickered, and pointed as they made their way past. All the previous humiliating moments in Stuart's life, combined and magnified one thousand times, would not come close to the embarrassment he felt at that moment.

"I suppose not. If he had determined our punishment was sufficient, I suppose he wouldn't have given us a lifetime of detention." Timothy pulled books out of his locker, each one thicker than the last. "Do you mind holding this for me for a moment?"

Timothy handed Stuart a calculus book roughly the weight of a small planet. "Wow, Timothy. What are you taking—high school-level classes now?"

Timothy closed his locker. His arms were filled with organic chemistry, biology, and trigonometry textbooks. "Heavens, no. This is a little light reading for my college placement exams. I want to start taking night classes at the junior college and need to bone up on these subjects during homeroom."

Stuart tossed the book on top of Timothy's stack and watched him struggle in vain to balance the leaning tower as it swayed from side to side. The stack of books crashed to the floor. The horde of students who saw the enormous mess on the floor refused to help.

As Stuart and Timothy reached for the books, a group of

jocks passed by. One stepped on Timothy's hand with his spiky cleats. Another took a running start and kicked the book pile across the hallway. They ran away laughing and slapping each other on the back.

Stuart sighed. "Some people, man. I tell you."

"Yes," Timothy said. "They are quite rude."

As they crawled across the hallway to collect the books, Stuart heard a soft, sweet voice above him. "Can I help?"

Stuart looked up to see an angel bathed in bright, white light. Madison. Madison Alberts was every middle school boy's dream: sweet, popular, cute as a button, and smart as a whip. She was about the only student that could even approach Timothy in terms of raw intellect, which irritated him to no end. And of course, Timothy's frustration tickled Stuart immensely. To top it off, she was about the only person who paid attention to Stuart in any meaningful way.

In kindergarten Madison had lent Stuart a purple crayon and allowed him to color with her, even though he was the class pariah. Moments like that and hundreds of others were the reason Stuart considered Madison the embodiment of all good, virtuous things in life. He was so smitten with her that he even liked the hideous, frilly pink pen that she kept tucked behind her perfect left ear. She had been wearing it for good luck all year, although it barely showed itself through her flowing, blonde locks.

Madison placed the last of Timothy's books on the now-uniform stack and helped Stuart to his feet.

Madison smiled. "Sorry about that. People can be so rude. If it were up to me, I'd sock them all in the gut. Teach them some manners."

"Y-y-y-eah." Stuart lost all sense of himself in her pearly white teeth.

The bell rang for class, and Madison snapped to attention. "Well, I'll see you in class."

With that Madison ran off and disappeared into a classroom down the hall.

"You can sock me in the gut any time," Stuart said.

Timothy gathered his massive stack of books and kicked Stuart in the shin, knocking him back to reality. "She's gone. And thank goodness. If she'd heard that, she would have most definitely run away." Timothy pushed the partially dazed Stuart down the hall. "Come on. Let's get you to class."

***

East Willow Middle School did not believe in separating students based on intellect or ability. They wanted students to exist in an egalitarian melting pot. Because of that, brilliant students like Madison and Timothy often co-mingled with the likes of Chet and his cronies. It was chaos.

Timothy and Stuart walked into the classroom to find it in shambles: students were yelling at each other from across the rows of uneven desks and throwing paper airplanes. Phones blared with incoming text messages.

Madison was the only student even half paying attention to the overwhelmed teacher. She sat quietly in the middle of the classroom, reading from her assigned textbook and waiting for the lesson to begin.

Stuart and Timothy took their seats toward the front of the class as the bell rang. "That will be quite enough of these shenanigans!" Ms. Reston said. She slapped the ruler on her desk, and the entire class shuffled to their seats to face front.

"Please take out a sheet of paper and a pen. We will begin the class with a pop quiz," Ms. Reston said.

Grumbles from around the class were followed by screeches and moans of "oh man," "really," and "this is completely unfair." However, there was only one screech that Stuart honed in on.

"Oh no. My pen!" Madison searched her hair to find the frilly pen she kept tucked behind her ear. She stood, checking frantically around her desk, picking up her books, and shaking out her folders. But the pen was nowhere to be found.

Ms. Reston called out from the front of the room. "Is there something wrong?

"My pen. My lucky pen. The one my mother gave me." Madison looked down.

Stuart refused to sit idle in this moment. His mind kicked into high gear; he mentally retraced every second of the morning. After a short time, Stuart snapped his fingers, hopped up from his desk, and darted out of the classroom.

Ms. Reston called after him. "Young man, you get back here right now!"

But Stuart was already out the door and halfway down the hall. Madison turned to Timothy. "Where is he going?"

"Your guess is as good as mine. Personally, I hope you don't find it. You could stand to lose a few more GPA points to me."

"Screw you, Timothy. I've got extra credit from journalism that just about has me caught up to you."

"Yes, well I suppose I'll just have to rely on my high school and college credits to secure the GPA crown again this year."

Before Madison could retaliate, Stuart burst back through the door gripping the pink pen tightly in his hand, victorious.

Madison's eyes lit up as she ran over and gave him a big hug. "Thank you, thank you, thank you. You have no idea how much this means to me. But how did you——?"

Stuart beamed with confidence as he handed the pen over to its rightful owner. "It was actually quite simple. Ever since the beginning of the school year, there's always been this subtle, little pink fringe that keeps the left side of your hair locked in place as you walk. When you helped Timothy pick up his books earlier, the pen was over your ear. But by the time you walked past the trash can outside of class, your hair had been set free and was bouncing as if something had come loose. So, I went back to the scene of the crime. Sure enough, your pen had fallen out and rolled under the trash can. Simple deduction."

"Well, you're my hero," Madison said.

Stuart smiled. He had experienced both the worst and best moments of his life in the span of a single school day.

Chapter 3

Damsel in Distress

Whipping rain poured down all around the Gumshoes headquarters. Inside, Stuart rested in front of the big-screen TV, watching cartoons and reading from his huge stack of Dan Dash pulp comics. He pounded his feet against the arm of the beat-up couch across which he was sprawled.

Timothy, meanwhile, sat behind his computer bank, diligently coding a program on his computer. The heavy clacking from Timothy's fingers across the keyboard pulsed and echoed above every other noise in the tree house, which drove Stuart bonkers.

In retaliation, Stuart whacked his feet harder against the

couch, which in turn drove Timothy batty and caused him to pound the keyboard louder and louder. Before long the noise grew so unbearable that neither could hear himself think.

Eventually, Timothy cracked. "ENOUGH!"

Stuart froze. After a long moment of silence, Stuart stood and bowed deeply. "I win. Admit it. "

"Yes, yes," Timothy said. "You've won Irritating Noises. That's all well and good as long as you please quiet yourself down."

"Come on. Don't be a sore loser. Just because you don't have the mental fortitude of a——"

"Excuse me? Compared to me you have the mental fortitude of an untrained chimpanzee."

"And yet, I won. What is that? Two hundred times in a row? Too bad, so sad."

Timothy turned back to his work without as much as a further grunt of acknowledgement. Stuart took that as a complete lack of respect and stomped over to Timothy. He peered over the monitor bank in a most annoying fashion. "Hey. No fair. It's no fun to gloat if you're not wallowing in it."

"Sorry I can't accommodate, but I've much work to finish," Timothy said.

"Too busy to wallow in frustration? This I've got to see." Stuart walked around the counter to look over Timothy's shoulder. Unfortunately for him, the entire screen was filled with nothing but indecipherable letters and numbers written in a funky computer language.

"What's that? Swahili?"

Timothy turned his monitor off and spun around to face Stuart. "That is none of your concern! For your information, it's for a program I'm working on."

Stuart tried to sneak around Timothy to turn the monitor back on, but he was impeded at every avenue. When Stuart zigged, Timothy zagged. When he ducked, Timothy rolled. Whatever Stuart tried, Timothy countered like a nerdy ninja. This was not the first time Stuart had attempted to disturb Timothy's work. As a result, Timothy had become exceedingly adept at defense.

"You know I can do this all night," Stuart said. "I'll just keep trying until you give up."

"You are persistently annoying. I have too much work left to accomplish to play this game with you any longer." Timothy turned back to his computer and flicked the monitor back on.

Stuart scratched his head. "I don't get it."

"It's not a magic eye, Stuart. No matter how hard you concentrate, an image will never appear out of the middle of the code. It doesn't work like that."

"Then how does it work, genius?"

Timothy pressed the space bar and the screen faded to black. "Please be careful. The user interface isn't complete yet, but I believe I've bypassed all of the catastrophic problems."

Stuart inched backward a few feet. "Maybe I'll stand over here."

The screen popped to life. A big, slimy-looking caterpillar inched its way across the screen, eating every piece of code in its path. The more it ate, the bigger it grew. Eventually, the caterpillar reached the center of the screen. It turned to look at Timothy, smiling a big grin. Timothy touched the screen to tickle under the caterpillar's chin like a proud parent. "Hello, little one."

"You've got weird tastes," Stuart said.

Stuart watched the caterpillar wrap itself in a cocoon of its own making. Once the caterpillar became fully enveloped, the cocoon pulsated.

"That's all it does?" Stuart said. "Pretty lame if you ask me."

"Give it a minute," Timothy said. "Wait until it reaches maturity."

"I've given it a minute already. One minute of my life that I'll never get back."

After pulsating for several mind-numbing minutes, the right side of the cocoon cracked open and a wing fluttered.

Immediately after, the left side of the cocoon broke open, and a second wing emerged and flapped. Finally, the entire on-screen cocoon exploded. Shards of cocoon burst across the screen so vividly that Stuart ducked to avoid the virtual explosion. The brown moth, at the center of the shards, flapped its wings while waiting for a command.

"All right, *that* was cool," Stuart said.

"If you think that's 'cool,' then watch this." Timothy feverishly typed on the keyboard. He quickly brought up the school's administration web page, which required a username and password to access records.

"You're stuck now," Stuart said.

A smug grin spread across Timothy's face. "Oh am I?"

With a couple more keystrokes he activated his moth, which seemingly ate the school's administration page.

Soon the log-in screen dissolved.

"Bingo," said Timothy.

Stuart looked. "*Access Granted. Welcome, Vice Principal Torres.* Wow!"

Timothy looked like a proud father. "I can access personal records, sick days, change grades, and even review the personal file for any student."

"Okay, now I'm sufficiently impressed," Stuart said. "Move over and let's see what this puppy can do."

"Oh, it's not a puppy. It's a *Semioscopis packardella*, or Packard's Concealer Moth to the layman. It's the next logical evolution to the traditional 'worm.' You see——"

"Dude, I don't care. I just want to play with it."

Stuart pushed Timothy out of the chair, cracked his knuckles, and took a seat in front of the keyboard. "What to do first."

"Just don't get us into trouble. There are still some bugs to work out." Timothy caught himself making a pun and chuckled. "Get it? Bugs. Because it's a bug."

Timothy's prattle gave Stuart an idea. He clicked onto the personal records panel and typed in Timothy's name.

"What are you doing, Stuart? This isn't funny."

"How about Dingus? Dingus Magee."

Stuart typed *Dingus Magee* into the name field where *Timothy Jorgenson* had been. "And let's make you a female."

Stuart clicked on the gender button and changed the sex from male to female. "Much better."

"Hey. Not funny. I have the appropriate anatomical requirements for my gender."

"And yet it says 'female' right here."

"Not for long!"

Timothy grabbed the keyboard at one end as Stuart latched onto the other. As the lightning violently crashed around them, they unintentionally smashed countless keys. Timothy knocked Stuart into the desk. The crash jostled the mouse, moving the cursor closer and closer to the submit button.

Timothy yelled when he noticed the cursor was hovering over the submit button. But that just startled Stuart. Stuart's resulting fall sent the monitor flying.

Timothy caught it, but something had come loose. The screen had gone white. "This is not good," Timothy said. "Did you click submit?"

"I don't know, dude. I was falling. Remember?"

"Let's hope not. Otherwise, I might be Dingus Magee forever."

Stuart brushed himself off. "Don't worry, man. Just use the worm thing again."

Suddenly, lightning crashed right outside the window, and the monitor turned blue. It read 'Fatal error'. Timothy's face contorted into a horrified mess. "Oh no. Quickly unplug everything!"

Timothy dropped to his knees and ripped cords from their surge suppressors. The computer began to grind and crunch.

Stuart ran around the room unplugging everything from the wall: the lights turned off, the TV went dead, the radio went silent, and finally the computers powered down.

Timothy and Stuart sat in the darkness huffing and puffing.

"Is it over?" Stuart asked.

"I believe so."

Stuart's breathing returned to normal. "Cool. Question? Why did we turn off the lights?"

"Everything should be safe as long as the power stays off for a few minutes. Then I will attempt a reboot and see just how much damage was done."

Another bolt of lightning struck. Thunder boomed through the headquarters, rattling the equipment. As the thunder shook the tree house, a girl's silhouette appeared in the window furthest from them. Another crackle of lightning revealed the familiar face of a classmate, sobbing under her drenched clothing.

Stuart cocked his head in disbelief. "Madison?"

Chapter 4

The Case

Madison sat on the couch, shivering under a thick blanket. Stuart sat next to her, concerned but without any words to comfort her. Timothy finished warming a coffee mug on a Bunsen burner and walked it over to Madison. He offered it to her, but she pushed it away.

"No thanks," she said.

"It's quite good. You need to increase your body temperature to stop the shivers and this will help."

"What is it?"

"It's my own special blend. It combines vitamins and minerals with an agent that keeps the molecules heated to a perfect eighty-three degrees, the ideal temperature for satisfying consumption."

"Sounds gross."

Stuart swiped the mug from Timothy. "It's actually awesome. It's like super-charged hot chocolate. Timothy's not really a salesman."

"You're sure it's not poison? There's no hydrochloric acid? I'm not going to turn invisible?" Madison asked.

Stuart shrugged. "Hasn't happened yet."

Madison grabbed the mug from Stuart's outstretched arm and took a hesitant sip. She licked her lips. Finally, satisfied she had not ingested anything harmful, she swallowed a larger gulp. "This *is* really good. Thanks."

"Now that your sobbing has ceased," Timothy said, "can you please inform us as to your plight? I lost your previous explanation in your tears."

"Yeah, you can start with telling us how you got up here," Stuart added.

"I climbed the tree," Madison said. "It's an old oak with lots of foot holds. Not that difficult."

Stuart looked at Timothy in disbelief. "Why didn't we think of that?"

Madison took a swig of the hot chocolate and collected herself. "Today, I stayed late at school to finish a story for the newspaper. The advisor drove me home because I missed the last bus. After he dropped me off, I walked to the door and found it unlocked. Not ajar, just unlocked. I know that my father had told me to call someone if that ever happened, but I didn't. I couldn't stop myself. I had to know, so I opened the door. When I walked inside, I saw everything was chaotic, as if there had been a huge struggle. Tables were overturned, our couch was flipped sideways, papers were strewn everywhere—even our TV was smashed to pieces."

Madison stopped as tears formed in her eyes. Stuart reached into the cushion of the couch and pulled out a handful of tissues. "They're clean. I promise."

Madison stared flummoxed for a moment before she accepted the tissues and wiped her eyes. "Thank you. I'm sorry. I'm just a mess right now."

"We're in no rush. Anything you need."

Timothy butted in rudely. "Well, I actually have a large project due tomorrow and I need to finish—OW!"

The shoe Stuart had thrown at Timothy hit him square in the nose and shut him up. Stuart turned his attention to Madison, who had just finished blowing her nose into the wad of tissues.

"Okay. I think I'm good now." She composed herself and continued. "I was really scared and I called out for my dad. He's always home by the time I get home from school. He doesn't like me coming home to a dark and empty house——"

"Then why didn't he pick you up?" Timothy said.

"He was supposed to, but Mr. Reed offered to take me home. He's that new English teacher they hired away from Braverton Middle. They made him advisor to the newspaper. I was alone for a little bit this afternoon while Mr. Reed ran errands. When he came back—I don't think he had expected me to be there, but I'd gotten caught up in finishing an article—I'd missed the last bus home. So I called my dad and asked him if I could catch a ride with Mr. Reed. He told me it was all right."

"Sounds logical, doesn't it, Timothy?" Stuart said.

"Yes, very." Timothy turned to Madison. "Please continue."

"So, the house was a wreck and I started calling out for my dad. I searched the whole house but nothing. He's been kidnapped. I know it. But I don't know why he was kidnapped. I'm so scared. I came here; I didn't know where else to turn."

"Well, we sure do appreciate you coming to us for comfort," Stuart said. "I just didn't think that we were that close."

"Oh, I'm sorry," Madison said. "I didn't come for that."

"Then why are you here?" Timothy said.

"I want you to take the case."

"Madison, most of our cases involve much smaller disputes—a lost cat or theft of the Sunday newspaper. This is more the jurisdiction of the police force."

"Oh, I called the police. They took my statement and they dusted or whatever it is they do. Told me they 'wouldn't rest until they found my father,' but I can't just sit and do nothing. I want to help. I need someone on my side working on this case."

"I'm sure there are much more qualified investigators in this town," Stuart said.

"Yes, I'm sure there are, but they charge an arm and a leg. I don't have that kind of money. And you're selling yourself short. I've seen you find stuff—like when you found my pen this morning. You're great, so I thought you'd help. You know, because you're my friend." As she said those last words, she placed her hand on Stuart's hand. He felt an electrical charge between them. "So, will you take the case?"

Stuart jumped on the chance. "Abso——"

Timothy interrupted. "Stuart, may I please have several words with you?"

"Can it wait?" Stuart said.

Timothy slammed his foot on the ground. "No. I'm afraid it cannot!"

"Fine. Jeez. Madison, just stay right here. This should only take a second."

***

Timothy waited, hot as a pistol, as Stuart walked toward

him. When he was within reach, Timothy smacked Stuart upside the head. "I cannot believe you were about to endanger our lives and the life of that nice girl in there just so you can hold her hand! Read my lips. We are *not* taking this case!"

"Listen, partner," Stuart said. "We have the most popular girl at our school sitting in our tree house and you want to turn her away?"

"Precisely. That's exactly what I'm saying. Thank you for understanding."

"I don't understand, Tim. I don't understand even one iota."

"Come on, Stuart. We investigate petty crimes. This is way out of our jurisdiction. Taking on a case of this magnitude is ludicrous and dangerous in every conceivable way. I refuse to be part of it."

"Really? You refuse? Well, let me tell you something. We get picked on every day in school. Madison is a serious babe and she seems to like us for some reason. Now, if we don't do this we'll not only piss her off, but we'll be stuck in a life of swirlies, wet willies, and wedgies forever. Madison is our way out."

Timothy pondered for a moment. "You make an interesting point. And I would prefer not to be tormented anymore. So you're saying if we help her, there is a chance that her popularity would extend to us?"

"At least we've got a shot at it. And it's the best shot we have. Now, I say we go inside and probe a little, get some answers, and if we think we can work the case, we'll investigate further. What do we have to lose?"

"Our lives," Timothy said.

"Quit being so dramatic."

***

Madison picked up a beaker full of purple liquid from behind Timothy's desk and stared at it. "This is so cool. Luminous phosphorus?"

Timothy ran over, grabbed the beaker from Madison's hand and placed it back in its proper place. "Yeah right," he said. "Like I plan on revealing my science fair project to you. Now, please desist in touching my equipment, Madison. I don't go to your home and read through your diary."

Stuart stared daggers at Timothy. "I have great news, Madison. We'll take the case!"

Timothy's ears perked up. "But that wasn't the deal. I didn't——"

Madison wrapped her arms around Stuart. "Oh my God. Thank you, thank you, thank you! That's so great."

After several wonderful seconds, Madison released Stuart. "Wow. Sorry about that. I'm not usually a hugger. And twice in one day. That's very unlike me."

Stuart tried to play it cool. "Oh, it's all right. I'll recover, you know."

"What do we do first?" Madison said. "Do you want to see my room? Interview the suspects? Gather the evidence?"

"First, I need you to calm down," Stuart said. "Before we get started, I need to ask you some questions about that night."

"Right. Of course. Ask away."

Stuart dug into his pile of comic books and pulled out a reporter's notebook. He flipped to an open page and pulled out a pen from inside a bag of potato chips.

"Now, you said that you called your father. What time was that?" Stuart asked.

"About six fifteen," Madison said.

"And it's roughly nine forty-five now," Timothy said. "Wow. This has been a late night for you."

"We have a deadline tomorrow and I had to make sure the layouts were right before we went to print."

"And when did Mr. Reed drop you off?" Stuart said.

"I don't know. Wait a minute." Madison flipped open her cell phone and searched her texts. "I sent a text to my dad to let him know I'd be home soon. That was around six thirty. I must have gotten home at around quarter of seven."

"So your dad was kidnapped sometime between six fifteen and quarter of seven," Stuart said. "That's a thirty-minute gap.

Did Mr. Reed come inside? Did you see him again?"

"No. When I turned around after walking inside, he was already gone."

"Is there anything else you can remember?" Timothy asked.

"I'm sorry. It was all a blur. I remember hearing from one of the detectives that it didn't look like anything was missing. They asked me to do a pass and nothing appeared missing to me, either."

Before she could elaborate further, Madison's cell phone rang. "Crud. It's my grandmother. I just ran out without telling her anything. I should go. Tell you what. Meet me at my lunch table tomorrow, and I'll try to piece everything together for you."

Neither Stuart nor Timothy had ever been asked to sit at the "popular" table before.

"Yeah, that would be cool," Stuart said.

"Great. See you then. Ciao."

Madison ran out into the rainy night. Timothy sidled up to Stuart. "This is a bad idea. I feel it in my tibia. That girl is trouble."

"I know. Isn't it great?" Stuart couldn't stop smiling.

***

Stuart walked home. He opened the front door and walked into the kitchen, which faced the street. A large bay window looked out to Timothy's house.

He sat down at the kitchen table as his mom finished serving dinner. Only the dark circles under her eyes belied her otherwise boundless energy and ceaselessly chipper attitude. She never left a hair out of place or a speck of dirt anywhere in the house, except for Stuart's disastrous room, which she had refused to enter for months.

"Good evening, dear. You were out late. You really should call if you're out late fighting crime." Stuart's mother set a plate of unappetizing meat in front of him.

Stuart lost every ounce of his appetite. "What's this? Buttchunk?"

"No, silly," his mother said. "Meatloaf."

"Yuck."

"It's your father's favorite."

"Yeah. I know. Where is he?"

Stuart's mother sighed as she grabbed her plate and sat next to him. "You know how he is. Work, work, work. But let's not talk about your father. Let's talk about you. Tell me about your day."

Stuart stabbed his meatloaf with a fork several times, trying to mobilize his appetite to no effect. "Mom, no offense, but can we get pizza?"

She looked down at her plate. Even she did not find the

meatloaf very appealing. "You know what? I think that's a great idea. More for your father, right?"

Stuart pushed his plate away. "Right. He can have as much of this as he wants."

His mother walked to the phone while Stuart looked wistfully out the window. Across the street, Timothy was eating alone and reading from a large textbook.

"Can we invite Tim?" he asked.

His mother barely had time to nod her head in approval before Stuart jumped out of his chair and rushed across the street.

Chapter 5
Popular Table

Timothy pushed his crust-filled plate away and patted his distended stomach. "That was spectacular. I don't think I could eat another morsel for at least twenty-eight million milliseconds."

"What is that? Twenty minutes?" Stuart asked.

"Try eight hours. By the time I wake up tomorrow morning, I'll be starving."

Stuart had barely listened to Timothy's answer before he turned to his mother. "Can we go up to my room?"

"Okay, but don't keep Tim here too late," she said. "It's a school night."

Stuart grabbed Timothy and jetted halfway up the stairs

before he called back over his shoulder. "Thanks, Mom."

***

Stuart's room made his side of the Gumshoes headquarters look pristine. Between the old food on his desk and the mold growing on heaps of discarded soda bottles, the smell of death and decay filled every inch of the tiny bedroom. Outside of a bed in the corner, a desk against the opposite window, and some Dan Dash posters, not very much else fit into Stuart's room; the piles of trash filled every nook and cranny. Even his mother refused to enter for fear of disease— or worse.

Stuart sat down at an ancient computer with a big, bulky old monitor and a blue racing stripe down the side. Timothy chortled as he looked over Stuart's shoulder. "Every time I see your computer, I die a little inside."

"I get that a lot. But it's got this awesome racing stripe down the side that makes it supercharged."

"State your evidence."

"Fact: racing stripes make everything faster and cooler. Hey, do you still have that bug—that wasp thing—online?"

"You mean my moth? Yes, I store an online backup of it on an international server for emergencies, but I haven't had a chance to modify it since our last encounter. It's still giving me some issues. Why?"

"We need to interrogate Mr. Reed tomorrow, and something's bugging me about him," Stuart said. "I poked around the Internets but didn't find anything. I need to get into his personal record."

"Internets? Every time I think you couldn't lower your intellect another iota, you outdo yourself. Don't you remember what happened last time?"

Stuart stared off into space for a good, long minute before he shook his head violently. "No."

"I sometimes wish for your ability to repress memories," Timothy said.

"All right Freud, just show me the bug. It's only going to destroy my computer if it doesn't work."

"That would be an upgrade. Move over. I'll get him."

Timothy scooted Stuart out of the chair, typing countless keystrokes in no time at all and digging deep into a server. The moth popped up and flapped its wings, ready to do Timothy's bidding. He leaned into the monitor and whispered into the moth's antennae. "You're going to be okay. Don't be scared. It will be okay."

"Are you really talking to a computer program?" Stuart asked. "You're a psychopath. It can't hear you. It doesn't have feelings."

Timothy ignored him. "I believe we are ready to proceed."

With that, Timothy flicked the keys with veracity. "Though I'm not what one would call a superstitious individual, you might want to cross your fingers."

Timothy pulled up the school's administration page. The moth burrowed inside. Soon, the log-in page melted into the access panel. Stuart shoved Timothy aside and began to maneuver around the site. The moth flew to the lower right corner of the screen and perched itself on the menu bar. "All right, let's see what Mr. Reed's personal file has to say."

Stuart clicked on Mr. Reed's permanent file and began to scan through it. Meanwhile, Timothy glanced down at the corner of the screen and noticed that the moth flapped its wings more violently than before, bucking and turning a bright shade of red.

"Hurry up," Timothy said.

Stuart tuned him out, carefully taking in every word of the document. As he scrolled through the file he reached a subfolder labeled CONFIDENTIAL in huge, bright red letters. He double clicked on the file, but it only initiated a dialog box requiring another password. "Timothy, I need your bug to work its magic again."

"I don't know about this, Stuart. It seems to be acting erratically. I believe we should close down this investigation until I can return the moth to peak efficiency."

"Dude, this is what I needed that stupid thing for in the first place. If you don't help me, it's all going to be for nothing. Your stupid fly will be useless."

Timothy sighed loudly and leaned over the computer. "Fine. But please be expedient about it."

After another flurry of keystrokes, the moth accessed the subfolder. Its job complete, the moth refused to settle on the corner of the screen. It flew erratically around the screen and flapped its wings, as if trying to avoid a predator.

"Can you get your bug to quit flying around so much?" Stuart said. "It's bugging me."

"No, I can't. It's in pain. This had better be worth it for the strain we're putting on him. Now hurry up."

"I think I've got something," Stuart said. "Mr. Reed was suspended just last year. Braverton Middle placed him on administrative leave for six months after he hit a student with his car. There was a huge lawsuit; he was fired and run out of town. East Willow Middle didn't steal him away. He was given a fresh start."

"He hit a student with a car? And they let him continue teaching?" Timothy said.

The moth radiated white light and flapped at supersonic speed around the screen. The information on the screen blurred as the moth flew around in a frenzy. "I think we should run," Timothy said.

"What's happening?" Stuart asked.

"SPIKE!" Timothy screamed.

Timothy yanked Stuart into the corner and pulled his mattress over top of them. Electrical charges flew until the monitor and the CPU exploded into the hallway with the speed of a jet engine, smashing through Stuart's door in the process and breaking his window.

Stuart pushed the mattress off and surveyed the damage. "What was that?"

"It would appear there are more kinks to work out with the system. When overworked, our little friend retaliates by emitting a high voltage spike into the system. Perhaps I should rethink making it sentient."

"Gee, you think!"

Stuart turned and saw his mother standing at the door to his room. She surveyed the damage. "I think it's time for your friend to go home," she said. "You will see him at school tomorrow."

Stuart looked at her. "I'm in trouble, aren't I?"

"Oh, you better believe it."

***

The next day at school, Stuart stormed up to Timothy's locker and slammed it shut. Timothy whipped around and greeted him with a smile. "Rough night?"

"Are you kidding me?" Stuart said. "I spent four hours cleaning up the mess your mosquito made. Now I've got detention *and* I'm grounded for the rest of eternity. I can't believe you can't get that thing under control."

"First of all, I told you that it wasn't ready and then I practically begged you not to use it," Timothy said. "Second, your mother's punishments are a joke. I'm quite sure you'll be able to continue as if nothing has happened."

"Yeah, well, you still stink. You should destroy that stupid thing."

Timothy gasped. "Not Spike. He's my friend."

"Spike? You named it? And worst of all, you named it after the explosion that destroyed my wicked-awesome computer with the cool racing stripe?" Stuart said.

"It seemed appropriate," Timothy said.

"You are an idiot."

"My IQ is significantly higher than anyone in this school. I promise you that."

"That's not what I meant. You're smart with this book stuff, but you are still an idiot."

"Perhaps you are correct because your logic has flown over my head completely."

As they bickered, Stuart caught sight of Mr. Reed ducking

into his classroom. "Come on," Stuart said. "We have work to do."

***

Mr. Reed's English classroom was a shrine to the written word; specifically, words written in a newspaper. Mr. Reed had chosen to hide the chipped stucco walls by covering them with thousands of newspapers, and barely a centimeter of the original wall remained. He had also placed huge tables against every wall, on which he displayed the posters and art work of his students like a proud parent.

From all outside accounts, Mr. Reed was a good, caring, funny man. He stayed late to help his students almost any day they needed tutoring, and he was always available to reach the high shelves that the other teachers could not. Yes, by all accounts he was a great guy, except for the little fact that he ran over a student not a year prior.

Stuart walked into Mr. Reed's classroom ahead of Timothy. "Hey Mr. Reed, can I talk to you for a second?"

Mr. Reed turned toward him, a jubilant smile across his face. "Of course. I'm always here to help out a couple of eager beavers. What can I do for you?"

"Well, I saw you get out of your car this morning and was wondering about it."

"Really? Are you thinking of getting a car? Aren't you a

little young?" Mr. Reed asked.

"No," Stuart said. "My mom's car was just totaled, and she's looking for something new. Yours looks cool. I want to tell her about it."

Mr. Reed picked up a large stack of papers out of his briefcase and distributed them onto all the desks. "Really? A 1974 Dodge Dart is cool? I think you kids are mistaken about what's hip. Plus, it's not much of a family car."

"Well, she's really cares about reliability, and it looks like it's lasted forever."

"Unfortunately, you'd be wrong there as well. I've only had that car for about a year, and it's constantly in and out of the shop. I recommend your mother try something a little more practical. Now, if there's nothing else, the bell is about to ring."

As if on cue, the bell rang and students started shuffling into their seats. Mr. Reed made his way to the front of the room. "I think it's time for you boys to head off to class."

"Right," Stuart said. "Thanks for your time."

But Timothy did not move. Instead, he could not help himself from asking the only question on his mind. "Just one more thing. Did you procure your automobile after you hit that student or before?"

The room fell deathly quiet, and Mr. Reed fumbled to construct a sentence. Finally, he pulled himself together.

"Follow me, gentlemen, into the hallway."

***

Mr. Reed pushed them into the hallway before letting go of his vice-like grip on their forearms. "I don't know what you heard, but those nasty ideas are where rumors get started. By tomorrow, I'm going to be known around here as the guy who hits kids with his car when they don't finish their homework on time."

"Wouldn't that be beneficial for you?" Timothy said. "It could help your students remain in line."

"Maybe for them, but not their parents. One kid goes home and tells a parent and I'm fired. Out of a job. And that's on your head."

"I'm very sorry for my friend's outburst," Stuart said. "We heard a rumor about your involvement in an accident with a student at Braverton Middle."

"Nothing was ever proven, and all parties are sworn to secrecy, so there's no way that anyone could have heard anything."

Timothy smiled. "So, you admit, then, that you were involved in such a case."

The second bell rang.

"You're going to be late. Watch yourself, boys." Without another word, Mr. Reed spun on his heels and walked into his classroom.

"This is why you're an idiot," Stuart said. "Now he's onto us."

"Yes, but he rightfully admitted his involvement," Timothy said.

"We didn't need him to admit anything. We had the case file. I just wanted to probe a little bit, get an in, and maybe have him drop his guard so that he'd reveal something that wasn't in the file. Now we're screwed."

"Oops."

"Come on, we have class. Let's hope that Madison doesn't kill us for interrogating her favorite teacher."

***

Timothy and Stuart walked into the bustling lunch room. Every faction was represented: losers, hippies, geeks, nerds, dweebs, bullies, outcasts, and the like. But in the middle, like a beacon of light in a dark forest, stood the popular kids' table. To be asked to sit there would change a kid's life forever. Anyone who sat with the popular kids would be treated differently. Not even Chet would dare mess with that. Typically, an invitation was next to impossible to obtain for anyone like Stuart or Timothy.

"You ready for this, Tim?" Stuart said.

"You mean the shame and ridicule that will surely occur

54

when we're rejected from their utopia? Yes, I believe I am."

"Then let's go."

Timothy and Stuart each took a single step, followed by another. Each step echoed in their brains. They felt every pair of eyeballs on them as they trudged past a table playing Magic and pushed past a table of outcasts hacking spitballs at each other.

As they approached the popular table, their breath became labored. Stuart turned to walk away. "I can't do this. It's too much pressure."

Timothy, however, in a show of unprecedented bravery, grabbed Stuart and spun him around. "No you don't. We are in this idiotic plan together. Now, let's embarrass ourselves."

As they passed the final gateway standing between them and the popular table, everyone in the lunchroom stopped to stare. For once, the attention was focused not on humiliation but on awed respect for their courage.

They arrived at the foot of the popular table, and the entire cafeteria let out a collective gasp. No other student had ever dared to venture that close without a formal invitation.

Stuart cleared his throat, and the busy chatter of conversation at the table suddenly died down. "Is Madison here?" he said.

Everyone at the table stared in amazement at their

stupidity before breaking out in a collective, murmured chuckle. Finally, Brad, the star center fielder—his golden locks bouncing as he laughed—raised his hand to silence the table. "She's getting her lunch. I think I speak for her when I say go away. You are not welcome here."

Stuart just about fell apart, but Timothy stood his ground. "We were asked to meet her during lunch today, and this is her table. Thus, logic states that we should meet her here."

Brad snorted dismissively. "Excuse me. I don't speak nerd. I speak awesome. And that's not what's coming out of your mouth right now. Now in five seconds, my lunch is going all over your face if you don't turn and walk away."

Madison saw Timothy and Stuart tuck their tails between their legs. She caught up to them before they left. "What's going on here?"

Brad pointed at Stuart. "These nerds said you wanted to see them. I was just putting them in their place."

"Brad, you suck," Madison said. "I did ask them to meet me here because we're friends." Madison cleared her throat and yelled loud enough for the whole cafeteria to hear her. "You hear that? These are my friends. If you screw with them, you screw with me. You got it?"

She glared back at Brad whose eyes darted to the ground. "Come on guys, let's go eat somewhere else before I lose my appetite."

Madison walked away. Timothy and Stuart followed in tow. Meanwhile, the entire cafeteria resumed normal chatter.

Chapter 6

Scene of the Crime

After school, Timothy and Stuart walked along the sidewalk toward Madison's house. Though they had never been to her house before, they knew what to expect just by the zip code. The neighborhood housed the town's most affluent residents— from the doctors and lawyers to the regional Emmy-winning meteorologist. If the eight- to ten-bedroom colonials were monsters, they would eat Timothy's and Stuart's homes, along with the Gumshoes headquarters, and still be hungry for dessert. In addition to large interior space, every home was enclosed by trees on three sides, which provided both precious privacy and amazing hiding places.

Stuart batted a low-hanging branch away. "All right Tim, here's the game plan. Don't speak. Let me do the talking and we'll be okay. I know Madison told us to go to her house after school, but we both know she just meant me. You two are like oil and water."

"I appreciate your confidence in my ability to be civil," Timothy said. "But how about you deal with your fixation on Madison, and let me worry about myself, okay?"

"Are you trying to tell me to mind my own business?" Stuart said.

"Absolutely."

"Look at you sticking up for yourself, buddy. I like it, and point taken."

As the Gumshoes drew closer, Madison's home rose over the horizon like a palatial estate. It dwarfed every other home on the already-lavish block. Every inch of its white-paneled exterior glistened in the afternoon sun.

The Gumshoes turned their attention away from the ostentatious house to the three lines of police tape forewarning all not to cross the path. Across the street from the house sat a squad car: two officers surveyed all of the comings and goings on the property.

Stuart stopped in his tracks in front of a lush row of bushes, which separated Madison's home from the neighbors, completely bamboozled by the presence of police officers. "I did not expect that."

"I'm sorry, you didn't expect that there might be police at an *active* crime scene? I think it's clearly evident that you are the idiot."

"Please. I've read the East Willow Police Department's operations manual cover to cover three times, and it clearly states that after twelve hours of constant surveillance, the squad cars are dismissed and only required to perform hourly sweeps of the premises."

"I'm surprised that you've read anything cover to cover."

"I'm going to spit in your lunch tomorrow."

"I'd like to see you try. Now, how the heavens are we going get inside with a police car watching every move we make?"

"That is a good question, my friend."

The bushes rustled and a soft, female voice emanated from within. "Maybe I can help."

"AHHH!" Stuart leaped into Timothy's arms, wrapping himself tightly around Timothy's neck.

Out of the rustling bush stepped Madison. She laughed as she brushed the brambles off herself. "You guys are a couple of pansies, aren't you? I should've hired someone else."

Stuart unwrapped himself from Timothy. "Please, if you could afford to hire better detectives, you would have."

"Plus, in order to hire someone, payment must be exchanged," Timothy said.

"Touché, Tim," Madison said. "You're all right. You know that."

"Enough with this jive." Stuart said. "Let's get down to brass tax. What are we doing here?"

"Are you kidding me?" Madison said. "This is the crime scene. You're a detective. So detect."

"Yeah, about that," Stuart said. "There's a cop car parked across the street. Not to mention the icky gross stuff inside."

"Well, the cops are an easy fix," Madison said. "Mrs. Bottoms from across the street just invited them to her place for a piece of her homemade blueberry cobbler. They've been drooling over it since she put it on the windowsill. So we won't see them for a while."

Stuart looked toward the police cruiser, and sure enough, the officers had vacated their post. "Fair enough. How are we going to get inside though, genius?"

Madison pulled out a key out of her pocket and dangled it in front of Stuart. "Hello? I live there, remember?"

"But that's an active crime scene," Stuart said. "Shouldn't we respect it?"

"Seriously, cream puff, how doughy are you?" Madison said. "What did you think we were going to do, sit around and play Miss Mary Mack?"

"N-n-no."

"Good. Then let's go."

Madison snuck through the bushes toward the side door of the house. In one swift motion, she lifted the police tape, unlocked the door, and slid inside. Then, she turned back to Timothy and Stuart and beckoned them forward. Stuart tried to follow, but his feet were glued to the pavement.

"Tim, old buddy," Stuart said. "Can you give me a little push? I seem to be frozen in fear."

"Only if you do the same for me," Timothy said.

"Deal."

***

Madison led the Gumshoes through an ornate trophy room to the living room. Stuart and Timothy admired the collection of antiques they passed, from Civil War muskets to Fabergé eggs—all encased behind thick, bulletproof glass. It was the fanciest room in which either of them had ever stepped foot.

Stuart immediately noticed that nothing seemed out of place. Clearly, Stuart surmised, if this were a robbery, every piece in this room would have been cleared out posthaste.

As the trophy room opened into the main living area, the devastation became immediately obvious. Madison's description paled in comparison to the actual destruction. An outside observer would more likely believe that a localized hurricane had blown through, rather than consider it evidence of foul play: the two front windows framing the doorway were smashed through, both couches were toppled, and the flat-screen TV had been not only ripped from the wall but also sent flying several feet across the room.

From the living room, the scuffle moved to the attached kitchen. The faux-marble countertop had been significantly dented and three silver bar stools were bent. Magazines, once stacked fifty high along the length of the counter, now completely covered the floor.

Stuart's eyes panned across the whole scene as he formed a mental picture of the attack. The victim had opened the cabinets along the back wall and flung the contents onto the kitchen floor, trying to slow down his attacker. "Well, at least there's no lack of evidence."

Bending down in front of the kitchen counter, Stuart picked up the magazine closest to his feet, *Better Housekeeping*, and halfheartedly flipped through it. Satisfied, he tossed it back on the floor and perused numerous other magazines. He determined that there must be at least thirty-seven different subscriptions strewn about the floor, which ranged from news and celebrity gossip to gardening and home repair.

He flipped through another magazine, but words and pictures were clipped out of nearly half the pages. "'How to Leave Your Bathroom Spotless.' Man, your father really loves magazines, but does he have to chop them up so much? It's hard to get invested in this article."

Madison snatched the magazine away and laid it on the counter. "They're not for him. Mr. Reed makes us go through all these magazines for stories and present a collage every month about what we find interesting—typefaces, grammar, and general trends in the marketplace."

"How is that journalism?" Timothy said.

"Well I think it's fun and informative," Madison said. "Dad's receptionist loves it, too, because we always give her the magazines the day after I turn the poster in." Madison took a few steps toward the staircase.

"Where are you going, Madison?" Timothy said.

"They won't let me stay here for obvious reasons, so I'm stuck at my grandmother's. I just need to go upstairs and get some clothes. I'll be right back. You guys keep investigating."

Madison disappeared upstairs. Stuart waited until he no longer heard footsteps on the staircase before he placed a hand on Timothy's shoulder. "Dude, this is way above my pay grade."

"That's what I've been trying to tell you," Timothy said. "I don't even know where to begin."

Stuart walked over to an upturned coffee table with a shattered glass face. "It's a shame. I bet all this cost a fortune."

"Well, I'm sure the cost is far less than the mental anguish of being kidnapped."

"True." Stuart bent down closer to examine the coffee table. He noticed a crimson discoloration glistening off one of the broken shards. Leaning in, he realized that it was a speck of blood. "Do you have any evidence bags, Tim?"

"Do I look like a medical examiner? I don't carry plastic bags except in my lunch."

"You're the crime scene investigator, man. You're the scientist. I point out the evidence and you bag it up. Just go look in the kitchen for something."

Timothy made his way into the kitchen, careful to tiptoe over any potential evidence. Meanwhile, Stuart crouched down on all fours and crawled toward the front door, his nose only centimeters off the ground as he scanned the carpet for clues. Before he discovered any new evidence, though, Timothy called out from the kitchen. "Stuart, you might want to come here."

"I'm busy," Stuart said. "Just bring any baggie—sandwich, trash, grocery. It doesn't matter."

"No, this is far more important than that," Timothy said.

With a deep sigh, Stuart pushed himself up and walked into the kitchen. "This better be good. You're ruining my process."

Stuart entered the kitchen and immediately recognized what required his attention: a pair of symmetrical scuff marks that ran the length of the kitchen, from the refrigerator to the counter. Stuart reached down and picked a small piece off the floor with his nail. He squeezed it between his hands. "Feels like rubber—probably from the sole of dress shoes. Somebody was dragged out of this kitchen, which means that the fight must have ended at the refrigerator."

Madison walked into the kitchen carrying a small duffle bag. Stuart turned toward her. "What kind of shoes does your dad wear?"

"You expect me to remember that off the top of my head? Hold on." Madison ran to the closet and pulled out a pair of shoes. "This kind."

Stuart grabbed the shoes from her. "Patent leather with dark soles. Yeah, that would do it all right. Madison, it looks like your father was dragged from the kitchen back into the living room. The fight definitely ended along the back wall of the kitchen by the refrigerator."

"That's good news, right?" Madison said.

Stuart walked to the refrigerator. "Possibly. It just doesn't make any sense; there are no doors in this room. Why would he run this way?"

"Maybe he wanted a snack," Timothy said.

"In the middle of a fight, Tim? That's ludicrous." Stuart bent down and looked into a small sliver of space between the counter and the refrigerator. Stuart could only see a glimmer from an object wedged inside. "Do you have a flashlight?"

Madison looked up into a now-empty cabinet. She looked down at the magazines strewn all over the floor. Brushing aside some magazines, she found the emergency kit under an issue of *Legal Ease*. She flipped it open and tossed the flashlight to an expectant Stuart. "Here you go. What are you thinking?"

Stuart shined the flashlight into the hole. "It's a jar. Something's stuffed inside."

Stuart reached out and grabbed for the jar. He struggled with all of his might, grasping, clawing for every centimeter. The tips of his fingers grazed against the lip of the bottle. He tried to squeeze his arm further into the hole, but the bottle remained just out of reach.

"Get me a knife or something," he shouted.

Madison surveyed the floor until she found a spoon lying on the ground. She picked it up and handed it to him. "This isn't a knife," Stuart said.

"What? They're dangerous."

Stuart rolled his eyes and grabbed the spoon. He latched it onto the jar and slid it, inch by inch, into his welcoming hand.

"Got it."

As he tried to pull his arm out to examine the jar, he realized he had wriggled, smooshed, and wedged himself so tightly into the crevice that he was stuck.

"Uh oh." He pulled as hard as he could, but the more he struggled, the more stuck he became. "Help me!"

Madison grabbed Stuart around the waist and heaved with all her might, but even their combined force would not dislodge him.

Before too long Madison stopped, wheezing and gasping for breath. "This isn't working. I have a better plan."

Madison released Stuart and made her way to the pantry. Stuart yelled in her direction as she searched the disorganized contents lying on the floor. "What are you doing?"

"Don't you trust me?" Madison reached down and popped up with a bottle of olive oil.

"Ah," Timothy said. "To coat the arm and reduce friction. Very smart."

"Then why didn't you think of it," Stuart bellowed. "Meanwhile, I'm still stuck!"

"Hold your horses," Madison said. "I'm coming." She opened the bottle and poured it down the crack. It oozed down and splattered onto Stuart's arm. "It's slimy. Gross."

Madison finished pouring the liquid and snapped the cap

into place. "Quit whining and pull."

Stuart heaved and his arm wriggled a bit. "Hey, it's loosening, but I could still use a good pull."

"My pleasure." Madison wrapped her arms around Stuart. "Ready? One. Two. Three. Pull!" They pulled with all their strength and *pop!* Stuart's arm came free. He lost his tenuous grip on the jar, and it flew through the air toward Timothy's outstretched arm.

Timothy almost caught the jar perfectly. Almost. It slipped through his hands and bounced once, twice, three times on the marble floor. Madison, Stuart, and Timothy, eyes shut and fists clenched in preparation for the sound of shattered glass, heard nothing after the third bounce. They opened their eyes. The jar lay motionless and unbroken.

Stuart crawled over to it. "Good job, butter fingers," he said to Timothy.

Stuart picked up the jar and stuffed his whole face inside to examine its contents. As he inhaled, his knees buckled and he became woozy. He fell to the floor with a loud thud, unconscious. The jar rolled out of his hands and across the floor as Timothy and Madison rushed to his side.

***

Madison dropped down and wrapped Stuart up in her arms. "Wake up, wake up. What do we do, Tim? Is he dead?"

Timothy bent down and checked Stuart's vitals. "He still has a pulse. But we have to move him. The officers outside must've heard that, and they'll be here any second to investigate."

Sure enough, they heard voices from outside as the officers ambled up the front stoop toward the front door.

Madison stuffed the jar into her duffle bag, slinging the bag over her shoulder before she grabbed Stuart's legs. "All right, you take his arms."

Timothy struggled as he picked up Stuart's arms. "He's heavier than he looks."

Madison picked up Stuart's feet and they carried him toward the trophy room as the officers began banging on the front door. "We have to move quickly," Timothy said. "These officers aren't going to be polite for long." They picked up their pace.

Sure enough, the officers banged louder. "Sir, you have five seconds to identify yourself before we break open this door."

Timothy and Madison moved as quickly as they could to the side door. Madison clicked the door open, and they hustled Stuart outside just as the front door opened and the officers burst in. "Freeze, nobody move." But there was nobody left inside. The side door had clicked shut a millisecond before the officers advanced to check the trophy room.

Outside, Madison and Timothy dragged Stuart past the thicket of bushes and down the street away from the house.

Chapter 7

Lou Lou Belle

Stuart lay on the couch at Gumshoes headquarters, still unconscious. Madison dabbed his head with a damp washcloth, occasionally stopping to dip it into a cup of water and wring it out.

"Maybe we should take him to the hospital," she said. "It's been over an hour and he's not waking up."

Timothy stood next to a centrifuge, holding an egg timer and waiting for the molecular compound in the rag to separate. Once separated, he could analyze the molecules under his IR spectrometer and discover the makeup of the mysterious liquid that had knocked Stuart out cold. "I don't find that to be wise," he said. "If this happens to be some illicit substance, we will surely be questioned. Besides, it's clearly not lethal."

"How do you figure that?" Madison said.

"Well, if your father's abductors had wanted him dead, there are certainly easier methods. Since they absconded with him, it's safe to assume that our concoction is not lethal. And in roughly forty-five seconds, we'll know for sure what is contained in its chemical makeup."

The egg timer dinged and Timothy turned off the centrifuge. He carefully placed the mysterious liquid inside the spectrometer so that its makeup could be analyzed. As he pressed start on the machine, Stuart started to moan and shift on the couch.

Exuberant, Madison shouted out to Timothy. "Tim! He's waking up."

"Fantastic," Timothy said. "Unfortunately, he's always quite irritable when he first wakes up, so I think I'll let you bear the brunt of his crankiness."

Stuart opened his eyes. The room was bright; it gave him a throbbing headache. "What happened?"

Madison handed him the cup of water she had used to dampen his head. "Here. Drink this. You were knocked unconscious from whatever was in that jar. Tim's analyzing it now to see exactly what's in it."

Stuart grabbed the cup and took a huge swig. "Thanks. I'm super thirsty and it feels like a million babies are kicking the inside of my skull." After swallowing a second gulp of water, chills ran down his back, from his spine to his toes. "This water tastes funny."

"It shouldn't. I've been using it to dab your forehead with this rag for an hour."

Stuart spit the water onto the floor and used the sleeve of his shirt to scrape his tongue. "Gross. Gross. Gross. You know what we use that rag for?"

Timothy barely stopped chuckling long enough to answer. "We use it to wipe the bird excrement off the sill and clean up spills around the lab."

Madison, horrified, chucked the rag out the window. "That is foul."

Stuart scraped his tongue vigorously. "Aw man, I can still taste it." In his fervor, his arm knocked the cup of water over. It spilled on the floor. "Hand me the rag, Madison," Stuart said.

"I don't have it," she replied. "I threw it out the window."

Stuart ran over to the window and saw the rag caught on a tree limb. "That was—now what am I going to do?"

Madison pulled a comic book, the Limited Edition *Dan Dash* #47, from the top of the stack next to the couch. "There's plenty of paper in here. Just use this."

Stuart dove and snatched the comic from her hand just as she began to rip the cover. He cradled the book in his arms like a baby. "Nooooo. Dan stopped the evil Fist D. Cuffs from blowing up the downtown express in that issue."

"What?" Madison said. "It's just a comic book."

Timothy perked up from behind his computer, where he was reviewing the printout from the spectroscope. "You've done it now."

"Excuse me?" Madison said.

Stuart placed the comic book down on top of the stack and smoothed out any new wrinkles Madison's handling had caused. "This is not just a comic book. Dan Dash is the greatest private investigator of all time. He's cool, collected, dynamite with the ladies, and always gets his man. Best of all, he doesn't need any of this technology. He uses his gut instincts—like a real, old-school cop."

Madison tried to process this foreign concept when Timothy shouted from across the room. "Chloroform!"

Stuart spun around to see Timothy smiling with glee. "Excuse me? Are you shouting random words to shut me up, buddy? Zucchini! I can do it, too."

"I finally finished my analysis of the bottle's contents," Timothy said. "The compound in question is none other than chloroform."

Madison shrugged her shoulders. "So, can't anyone buy chloroform anywhere?"

Timothy vehemently shook his head. "No. That's a common misconception because villains in movies and television shows always seem to have easy access to it. However, it's actually quite hard to obtain. You must have a license from the state in order to buy it, and it's very strictly regulated. It should not be very hard to obtain a complete list of buyers from the past month or so."

"Great, Tim. Stay on that." Stuart turned to Madison. "Meanwhile, do you think we could get into your father's office? There might be a clue there as to who might want to hurt him."

"Good idea, Stuart," Timothy said. "While you and Madison attempt to infiltrate the office, I will compile a list of suspects."

Stuart held out his hand toward Madison. "Shall we?"

"Lead the way." Madison smiled coyly as she took his hand.

***

The exterior of her father's office building was a bland gray, concrete façade. With a large number of big, darkly tinted windows, the building looked like thousands of other office buildings. Stuart didn't care about that though. All he thought about was how pretty Madison was and how his luck had changed.

Once they reached the door to her father's office, Madison stopped him. "My father's name is Sylvester. You'll need to know that if you pretend to be my friend. Got it?"

Stuart nodded. "Yeah, no problem. Sylvester."

"And there's one more thing. The secretary, Lou Lou Belle, can be a little much to handle. She's a dear, but just try not to be swept into her craziness."

"You're talking to me, Madison. I'm a rock."

Madison smiled as she patted him on the cheek. "Yes, you are."

"I mean how bad could she be?" Stuart asked.

As she opened the door to the office, Madison looked back over her shoulder at him. "You'll see."

Stuart stepped over the threshold. Immediately, he realized that Madison had actually undersold Mr. Albert's ebullient secretary, Lou Lou Belle. She was so positive and full of life that it seemed as though a bright ray of sunshine had enveloped him.

"Alberts and Mitchell, please hold. Alberts and Mitchell, please hold. Alberts and Mitchell, please hold." Lou Lou Belle repeated the greeting over and over with such perfect pitch and consistent delivery that callers could easily mistake her for an automated machine.

"Okay," Stuart said. "I get it. I'm tired just looking at her."

Madison jabbed him in the ribs. "Shhh."

"Alberts and Mitchell, please hold. Alberts and Mitchell,

please hold. Alberts and Mitchell, please hold. Yes, I'm sorry, but Mr. Alberts is unavailable. Yes. You have a nice day as well." Lou Lou Belle kept up this frantic pace until she saw Madison. She immediately slammed down all of her phones. Even as the chorus of ringing continued around her, she remained completely focused on the young lady and her Gumshoe protector.

"Oh, my sweet dear," Lou Lou Belle said. "How are you?"

Madison propped her arms on the reception desk. "I'm doing all right, considering, Lou Lou Belle. Yourself?"

"Oh. I, well, I'm keeping busy. Every time I stop, for even a second, to think about it, I start to cry." Lou Lou Belle could not hold back the tears; her blood-shot, tired eyes were blurred behind a pool of grief, and the layers of concealer she had applied that morning washed away.

Stuart noticed a box of tissues. He grabbed it and offered the tissues to Lou Lou, who pulled four out and used them to blot her eyes.

Lou Lou took a deep breath and calmed herself down enough to speak again. "Thank you, young man. Are you here protecting little Miss Madison?"

Stuart shook his head. "No, ma'am. I'm investi——"

Madison clasped her hand over Stuart's mouth. "This is Stuart. He's my friend. You know it's hard to be alone after——

"

Lou Lou Belle nodded in agreement as she blew her nose with another handful of tissues. "Oh, don't I know it. It was hard for me to even get out of my house and away from my cats this morning. But I've been here every day since those doors opened—ten years ago next week—and I'll be darn tootin' if I miss a day at this office in its hour of need."

"That's noble of you, ma'am," Stuart said.

"I have to ask you something, Lou Lou," Madison said.

"If it's in my power to give, you'll have it," Lou Lou Belle said.

"Do you think it would okay if we go into my father's office and get a picture of him?"

Lou Lou Belle looked her up and down, skeptical. "Surely your grandmother has lots of pictures of your father lying around the house."

"Yes, but she doesn't have anything from the past decade, Lou," Madison said. "If I wanted to see my dad as a kid, sure, I'd have tons to choose from. But nothing recent. You know he's a workaholic, and we're not the best with pictures. I know he keeps some in his office, though."

Lou Lou Belle smiled at her for a long, endearing moment before nodding. "Of course, dear. You know, sometimes I sit in the middle of the room, remembering what a wonderful man your father was."

Lou Lou's attention turned back to the chorus of ringing phones. She quickly straightened herself up and readied herself to work again. "Now, if you'll excuse me. We have some very scared and nervous clients, and I have to keep the ship sailing straight. You take all the time you need."

"Thanks, Lou Lou. You're the bestest."

"The bestest bestest, and don't you forget it." Lou Lou Belle seemingly answered four phones simultaneously. "Alberts and Mitchell, please hold. Alberts and Mitchell, please hold."

***

Timothy paced back and forth in front of his bank of computer monitors. Spike, perched on a dialog box in the center of the screen, followed Timothy with his eyes. "Okay my moth friend, you might be slightly temperamental, but I am your father, and you must do as I say."

Timothy sat down at the computer. "I need you to grant me administrative access to every postal shipping company in the United States."

Spike's wings fluttered nervously. "I know it's a big job, but you can do it. I've decreased the decryption sensitivity that overloaded the memory, so if you could please be so kind as to not freak out on me, I would be exceedingly grateful. Let's just take it one at a time."

With a couple more keystrokes, Spike began to burrow into the UPS mainframe. Timothy crossed his fingers and leaned back in his chair to wait.

***

Mr. Alberts's office was adorned much like his house. Unlike the sparse decorations that surrounded Lou Lou's desk, Mr. Alberts's tastes were more refined, which carried through to his ornate style. Along every wall, carved-oak bookshelves brimmed with leather-bound books. A bay window—the only one in the entire office park—allowed the sun to streak through on the left side of the room. His desk, made from a 2,000-year-old maple tree, screamed class and elegance. Behind the desk was an antique grandfather clock, which had passed from father to son for three generations. It kept perfect time.

Outside of a computer, desk calendar, and appointment book, only picture frames adorned his desk. Madison had made each picture frame from macaroni shells. The pictures themselves depicted special events in their lives together. Mr. Alberts kept each picture as a keepsake; it was a concrete reminder to Madison that her father cherished her.

"All right, Stuart," Madison said while locking the office door, "we're looking for anything that could implicate somebody in Dad's disappearance. We don't have much time."

Stuart rummaged through the nearest bookcase. Madison walked over to her father's desk. As she picked up a picture of their camping trip, a piece of macaroni broke free and fell to the floor. In the picture Madison's dad held her upside-down with one arm and held up a trout in the other. He wore a big smile on his face. As Madison stared longingly at the image of happier days, a single tear fell down her cheek.

"Are you okay?" Stuart said.

Madison wiped her eyes with her sleeve. "Yeah. I'm fine."

But Stuart sensed that she might be a little less than okay. He walked over to her and wrapped his arm around her. She rolled toward him and buried her head into his chest, sobbing at the thought of losing her father.

"Hey, it's okay. It's okay. Just let it out." He did not attempt to ease her pain with any more words; instead, he was content to rub her back until no tears remained. Eventually, she pushed off and left a stain comprised of tears, snot, and makeup, which completely destroyed his shirt. But he did not care; he was just happy to be that close to her for even a moment.

"Sorry, I lost it for a moment," Madison said. "I'm not usually that blubbery."

"No problem," Stuart said. "Just don't let it happen again." He chuckled uncomfortably. "I'm just kidding. You can do that as much as you want. I mean your dad—well, you know. But the best defense against those bad feelings is to get the bad guys. There's got to be evidence here somewhere."

Madison nodded and placed the picture down on the desk, turning it away from her misdeeds. "Sorry, Dad. I know you wouldn't approve of me as a criminal, so you'll have to sit this one out."

***

Timothy anxiously spun a penny on his desk while he watched the seconds tick by. Spike had already eaten through the UPS, FedEx, and DHL mainframes. Timothy was starting to lose hope the package had not been sent by any of the major US couriers.

Spike burst through the browser window after successfully hacking into the United States Postal Service mainframe. Exhausted, the moth settled on the top of the browser window. "I know that was a tough one, buddy. Rest there for a minute."

As Timothy began digging into the shipping records, Spike turned a menacing shade of red. Within a few seconds, Spike quickly became glowing-white hot, ping-ponging across the screen at lightning-quick speed. Timothy had no choice but to manually shut down the browser program in an effort to calm Spike down. Low and behold, it worked. Spike settled harmlessly at the corner of the menu bar.

Timothy opened Spike's programming software and

searched the diagnostics for a clue regarding the recent abnormalities. "Five million lines of code and I'm looking for one anomaly. Think, think, think. It's as if I'm trying to find a one special piece of hay in a haystack."

Timothy beamed. "Oh my goodness. Could it be this simple?" He typed a couple of keystrokes and reworked three lines of code.

"You were just a memory hog, weren't you? Well, that should stop you from destroying my computer. Feel better now?"

Spike nodded and fluttered happily around the screen.

"Well, of course you do. Your memory consumption quadrupled every fifteen seconds until you literally ate every process and failed my system. You should feel better from here on out. Yes, you should."

Timothy scratched the monitor right under Spike's chin, and Spike flapped his wings happily.

"Now, let's get to work."

***

Stuart and Madison sat crisscross applesauce on the floor of her father's office. After searching through every nook and cranny without any trace of a clue, they decompressed with a well-deserved break. Unfortunately, their fruitless search had brought them no closer to finding her father.

Stuart leaned back, and his eyes caught a glimpse of the grandfather clock. "Wow. We've been here three hours. It's a good thing Lou Lou's busy or she would have realized it doesn't take this long to snatch a picture."

"I can't take it anymore. Everything we do just leads to a dead end." Madison, frustrated, banged her head against the wooden floorboard. *Thunk!* The wood sounded hollow. She rubbed her head. "Wait. That wasn't right."

She knocked her fist against the floorboard. *Thunk!* She moved her hand along the floorboards, both parallel and perpendicular to the hollow-sounding one. *Thwip! Thwip! Thwip! Thwip!* All of them made the exact same sound. Then, she knocked again on the first floorboard. *Thunk!* "There's something weird about this one. Is it hollow? Help me lift it. There might be something underneath it."

Together, they dug their hands under the floorboard and pried it up with all of their might. Stuart grunted and struggled to raise the floorboard higher as Madison reached into the hole and felt around. Finally, she rooted around deep enough and grabbed onto something. She pulled out a swath of red file folders that had been bound together with a rubber band. "Got it."

As Madison slid her hand out of the hole, the floorboard smacked closed and sent a reverberation through the office.

They heard Lou Lou's chair creak as she stood and walked toward the door.

"Are you kids still in there? It's been a long time. Are you causing problems?" Lou Lou jiggled the locked doorknob. "That's it. I'm coming in! Just wait until I find the key."

Stuart stood and pulled Madison up. "I don't get it," she said, "these look like standard case files. Why would my dad need to hide them?"

Stuart ran over to the window and pushed it open. "I don't know, but we can figure it out after we escape. Luckily, we're on the first floor."

Stuart helped Madison out the window before he hopped out, shutting the window behind him. As they ran across the street, Lou Lou flung open the door to the office and rushed inside to find nothing out of place. "I must be going insane."

As she walked toward the window, the phones caught her attention and she ran to answer them. "Alberts and Mitchell, please hold."

Chapter 8
Red Files

Barry's Diner defined what East Willow folks know as downtown. The three-block area, East Willow's main street, would not even take up a single block of Times Square. However, the town seemed perfectly at peace with its size, and Barry's Diner was its cornerstone. Middle- and high-school students frequently enjoyed dinner there—to celebrate a good grade or a win after a big game, or to avoid being scolded by an irate parent. Barry, both the diner's namesake and the short-order cook, did not much mind why the students came to his restaurant, as long as they spent money. Longing for what he referred to as the "good ole days," he decked out his restaurant with old-fashioned juke boxes at every table, roller skating servers, red vinyl seats, and a soda jerk that delivered the best treats in three counties.

Madison and Stuart sat at the booth in the furthermost corner of the diner, trying to avoid prying eyes as they scattered her father's case files across every inch of the table.

A server skated up and stopped in front of them. "Can I get ya'll anything, or are you still happy with the water?"

Madison looked up from one of the files and shook her head. They had scanned every piece of paper in those files twice with no luck. "You could make my eyes stop burning, Muriel. But otherwise, we're good."

Stuart, however, heard the exhaustion in her voice and decided to cheer her up. "Actually, I think we'll have a banana split. Thanks so much. And Muriel, make it the Monster."

"Excellent," Muriel said. "And I'll be right back to fill up your water glasses."

Muriel rolled away, and Madison glared at Stuart. "What are you doing? We have a lot of work to do, and we don't have time to be eating ice cream."

"Madison, you've got to relax," Stuart said. "We've been sitting here for over an hour. We've been concentrating so hard I'm nearly cross-eyed. I need to relax and so do you."

As Stuart crammed the files back into their respective folders, Madison struggled with all of her might against him. He ripped the papers out of her hands. "See, isn't that better?"

Madison refused to answer until she had locked eyes with the biggest banana split she had ever seen in her life.

"There you go, hon," Muriel said, setting it down on the table. "Nice to see you two enjoying yourselves. You were about to lose your minds if you looked over them papers any longer."

Stuart beamed with pride as Muriel refilled their water glasses. "That's what I said."

"Great minds think alike." With a wink and smile, Muriel slid herself toward another table and left Madison to eye over the confection, barely able to see Stuart over the heaping sundae.

Without wasting another second, Stuart gripped his spoon and scooped a big chunk out of the top so he could see Madison better. "Dig in," he said, his mouth full of sugary goodness.

Madison picked up her spoon and dug into the enormous sundae, careful to take symmetrical bites so that it would not crash down on top of her. As the effect of the chocolate, vanilla, and caramel washed over her for the first time in days, she forgot that her father was missing and lost herself in a moment of pure bliss. "This is so good."

"I told you," Stuart said. "So, how's—Mom?"

"Look, Stuart, I appreciate the gesture, but you don't have

to make small talk. I'm perfectly content just to eat my ice cream in peace."

"I know. But, I mean, we've known each other since kindergarten, and I think it's safe to say I don't know much about you."

"Really? Because I know a lot about you. I mean you're a private investigator; don't you have eyes and ears?"

"Well, of course. But, I mean, I'm not a snoop. I give people their privacy."

"Really? Since when? I remember when you recounted for the entire class what Roger Jenkins did one weekend—just by looking at a stain on his shoe. Those kind of observational skills, and you really know nothing about me?"

Stuart sighed. "All right, fine. I know a lot about you. Come on, you're the most popular girl in school. I just wanted to hear it from you, okay? Like we're really friends."

Madison took another bite of the sundae. Then, she placed her hand over his. "We are friends, Stuart. You don't have to worry about that. My mom, I don't know. She's enjoying India or Pakistan or Lebanon, or wherever she is. She bailed on us. I get a postcard sometimes, but I just toss them in the trash."

"I'm sorry. I didn't know. I just thought——"

"It's all right. Nobody knows, really. Usually it's the top thing on my mind, but since my dad went missing, I guess I should just be glad my mom's safe, right? I mean, I assume she's safe."

Madison stopped for a second, her momentary elation replaced by the crippling thought that she did not know whether either of her parents were alive. Stuart, noticing Madison's change in demeanor, balanced his spoon on his nose. "Hey, look at this!"

Madison glanced up, unable to decide whether to be angry at Stuart's lack of compassion or happy that he was trying hard to cheer her up. Before long, she settled on the latter and laughed to herself before scooping up another spoonful of ice cream.

The bell above the diner door rang out and Brad entered, followed by a small group of his baseball cronies. Madison, embarrassed, quickly slid her hands away from Stuart's.

They strutted over to Madison. "Well, well, well, look at Madison out on a date. No wonder you're in the back nook. I'd want to keep this on the DL if I were with this nerd, too."

Madison turned red in the face. "Listen, we are *not* on a date. No offense to Stuart, but there's no way that would ever happen."

Stuart wanted to die of humiliation, but instead he stood up, trying very hard to hide his broken heart. "Good friend, Madison. Really cool."

Stuart stormed out of the diner. Brad snorted as he watched Stuart slam the door behind him. "Uh oh. Looks like trouble in paradise."

Madison smiled coyly as she rose to meet Brad's gaze. "Oh, Brad. You're such a stud. I just love it when you pick on the little people. Makes you look like such a man." Madison stroked Brad's arm as she inched closer to him.

"Yeah?"

"NO!" Madison pushed Brad away, picked up the heaping sundae and threw it over Brad's head, which drenched him in gooeyness from head to toe and sent him flying backwards into the counter. She tossed down twenty dollars onto the counter, scooped up her dad's files, and hurried to catch up with Stuart.

***

Stuart was already halfway down the block when Madison exited the diner, and he moved ever faster away from her.

"Stuart, wait!"

"Why? So you can mock me some more?" Stuart screamed.

Madison jogged to catch up with him. "Come on, Stuart. That's not fair. If you were any other guy, I would've said the same thing."

"Sure. I'm sure if you were sitting with Brad and I came in and said the same thing, you would've gotten all embarrassed."

Madison caught up to Stuart. She grabbed his arm and spun him around toward her. "First of all, yuck. Brad is a total tool. Second, yes, I would have gotten embarrassed because I've never been on a date before and it's embarrassing. Third, you never would've said that because you're a nice guy."

Stuart stopped fuming and cracked the smallest of smiles. "It's very hard to stay mad at you when you say stuff like that. Do you know that?"

"Yes, I do. I'm adorable. Now walk me to my grandmother's house."

"As you wish." Stuart offered his arm to her. Madison graciously tucked the files under one arm and slid her other arm through the nook in his.

Madison laid her head on Stuart's shoulder, and she looked up at the trees. "It's hard to believe that Brad and I are even part of the same species."

Madison's words resonated with Stuart, and a kernel of an idea formed into a brilliant one. He stiffened and shook Madison's arm loose. "Madison. You're a genius. Let me see those case files."

Madison pulled the case files from under her arm and handed them to Stuart. "Really? Because we were kind of having a moment."

"I know and I'll kick myself later, but I just had an amazing thought. We spent so much time focusing on each case, we didn't think about how they related. What if there's something all of these files have in common, and that's the reason your father hid them."

Stuart rifled through the folders. "In every one of these cases, the complaints against your father led to the plaintiffs filing lawsuits against him personally. I bet if I give these to Timothy, he'll be able to find something on one of these plaintiffs that'll lead to a suspect."

"That's almost worth ruining a moment for," Madison said. She wrapped her arm back under Stuart's, and they strolled away.

***

Stuart slammed the front door. The sound alerted his mother, who called out from the kitchen. "Dinner's on the table. Meatloaf. We've got to finish it."

"Is Dad here?" Stuart asked.

"Sorry, sweetheart," his mother said. "He has to work late."

"I'm not hungry. I'll be in my room."

She poked her head out into the hallway. "You sure, sweetheart? It's warm."

"I don't feel so good, and I have a bunch of homework."

"Okay, honey. Feel better. You want me to bring you up some aspirin?"

"No, ma! I'm fine."

He locked the door to his room. The charred remnants of his desk, a rusty folding chair from the attic, and the singed mattress were all that remained from the explosion.

Stuart plopped down on the chair and laid his head on the desk. A light flickered on from Timothy's house across the street. Timothy opened his window. He waved his walkie-talkie frantically in the air. Stuart pulled his walkie-talkie out of his book bag and clicked it on. "I thought these were antiquated," Stuart said.

"You are the one who constantly requests that we use arcane technology," Timothy said. "I assumed you would be ecstatic at my embracing this device. I must say it has grown on me."

"Told you. Over."

"I found out something about your red folders. I hacked into the police database and cross-referenced them through several courts and offices of the county clerk. One of the defendants, Dr. Otis Howard, happens to run the research and development program at Thomas Pharmaceuticals."

"Come on, man. While I've got my health. Over."

"Patience is a virtue, Stuart. Where was I? Oh, yes. I was just about to reveal that Thomas is the fourth-highest manufacturer of chloroform in the contiguous United States. It shouldn't be a problem for Dr. Howard to retrieve some of the chemical. Additionally, he had sent several death threats to Mr. Alberts's home and office."

"That's great news," Stuart said. "We'll tell Madison in the morning. We finally have a solid lead."

Chapter 9

Idiot Detective

Unlike Mr. Alberts's palatial estate, Madison's grandmother lived in a modest, two-bedroom home, which was near Stuart and Timothy's neighborhood. She had lived in the same home for most of her adult life, raising her family there. Every deformation, bruise, blemish, and ding in the house held a story to her. Her home was not flashy, but it certainly held a lifetime of character.

Madison walked down the creaky, wooden stairs of her grandmother's house and heard a gruff voice—the detective who oversaw her father's case—coming from the kitchen. She stopped in her tracks and leaned over the banister, eavesdropping on the conversation between her grandmother and the detective.

"This is truly delicious pie, Mrs. Alberts," the detective said. "My wife would kill me if she knew I was off my diet. But between you and me, if she cooked like this, I'd probably be fifty pounds heavier."

Madison sneered as she heard the guttural laugh of the detective combine with the piercing cackle of her grandmother's squeal. As the laughing subsided, Madison heard her grandmother take a seat next to the detective. "That's very kind of you, Detective. I haven't laughed a good laugh since—well, you know."

"Yes, ma'am. You can call me Josiah. I'm afraid I am not the bearer of good news, in all honesty."

Madison stood on point as she leaned closer, not wanting to miss a word. However, her foot slipped, and all of her weight landed on a broken stair, which let out a mournful creak.

Madison's grandmother clammed up. She spoke barely above a whisper as Madison gingerly crept down the stairs toward the kitchen. "Hush now," she said. "My granddaughter is about ready for school, and if she hears any of this, she'd just fall apart."

Madison had heard enough. She leaped down the remaining stairs and stomped into the kitchen.

She saw her grandmother sitting across from the detective

at the small, circular breakfast table, which was covered with a cloth frayed around the edges.

Madison's grandmother whipped around toward her. "Good morning, dear. Can I get you some breakfast?"

"Why is he here?" Madison said. "You know I don't want him anywhere near me."

"Now, he's just doing his job. Came to give me an update on the case."

"And why didn't you tell me? Don't you think I'd like to know how my own father's case is progressing?"

The detective placed his fork down, next to his piece of partially eaten cherry pie, and looked up at Madison. The first thing she saw was the bushy cookie-duster mustache that hung over his mouth and hid his jaw. Madison looked at his long, hard face: he did not look like someone who was prone to giving good news. A classic brown fedora rested next to his plate, and a matching trench coat covered the back of his chair. She couldn't resist thinking that this man sitting across from her grandmother was Dan Dash in the flesh, down to the revolver he kept tucked into a shoulder holster.

"I think I can answer that," he said. "I know you don't like me, so I was trying to respect that. Maybe I was wrong, but your grandmother and I both thought that was best, given the circumstances."

"Well, I heard everything up until now," Madison said. "So if you've got something to say about my dad, then I have a right to hear it."

"But child, I don't want to upset you," her grandmother said.

"I'm already upset," Madison said. "My dad's gone. If this is the man who's going to bring him home, then I want to know what he has to say." She folded her arms menacingly. "So, detective, is this what you do? Track down missing people?"

"Not most of the time. We are a really small force, so we all do just about everything. However, I've tracked down a couple people in my day."

"I see. So, in your expert opinion, where is my father?"

The detective took a deep breath. He swallowed loudly as his eyes dipped toward the floor. "We don't know."

Tears welled up in Madison's eyes. "Have you made any progress?"

"As I was about to explain to your grandmother, we have every resource at our disposal to track down your father. But like I said, we are a very small force. Every piece of evidence has to be sent out to a lab. Every detective is working thirty-plus cases. We just don't have the manpower we need—I promise you that we're doing all we can, but as of right now, we have nothing solid."

Madison did not have the strength to look at him for another second. As she turned to leave, he called after her. "I will continue to work for you until your father is found—one way or another."

Madison spun back around. "What do you mean, one way or another?"

"Poor choice of words."

"You think there's a chance that he could be—dead?"

"Absolutely not."

"But that's what you said. You said you'll look for him until you find him one way or another, which means he could be dead when you find him. Right?"

He stared in silence, nary a comforting word to be found.

"Right?" Madison asked again.

"I'm afraid that is always a possibility."

"Well, let me tell you, Detective, it doesn't give me a whole lot of comfort if you find my father dead. So, how about you get back to work instead of eating my grandmother's pie."

Madison ran out of the room. Her grandmother yanked the detective's pie away before he could take another bite. "First day on the job? Because you sure scared my little girl like someone who doesn't have a clue about what he's doing. I hope you're a better detective than you are a conversationalist."

Josiah stood, placing the fedora on his head. "Me too," was all he could muster.

***

Madison pushed a stack of books into her locker. She could not pretend that today was just another day at school—she could not get the conversation with the detective out of her head. Finally, the anger that had been welling up in her burst out. Tears streamed down her face as she repeatedly pounded her fists against the locker with all the ferocity she could manage. Finally, her knuckles bleeding, she stopped.

After she wiped the tears away and composed herself, she turned and saw Mr. Reed standing in front of his classroom with a box of tissues. "You need one?"

Madison nodded her head and walked into Mr. Reed's empty classroom, grabbing the tissue box as she passed him.

Madison sat in the far corner of the room, as far from the prying eyes of students as she could get without falling out the window. "Can you turn the lights off, please? I don't want anybody seeing me like this."

Mr. Reed flipped off the lights, and Madison cried vigorously into a handful of tissues. She blew her nose and placed the tissues on a nearby desk. Mr. Reed walked over and grabbed them. "I'll take those."

"T-t-t-thank you," she said.

"You know," Mr. Reed said, "it can be hard enough growing up without having to deal with everything you've had to go through. If you need anything, you can come to me."

The bell rang and the hallway scuffle increased. "Thank you. I appreciate it. I should be going to class."

"You sure you're all right? I can write you a note."

"I think we all know I'm not all right," Madison said. "But I'll get by. I don't want any special treatment."

Mr. Reed smiled. Madison stood and wiped her sniffling nose on her sleeve. She picked up the tissue box. "Can I have these?"

Mr. Reed nodded. Madison stuffed the tissue box into her backpack and walked away, flicking the lights on and tossing her used tissues into the trash can.

***

Madison, puffy eyed but composed, opened her locker and pulled out her books for first period. She slammed the locker closed in a final fit of anger and looked up to see the smiling faces—well, one smiling and one daydreaming—of Timothy and Stuart.

"We have news," Stuart said.

"Well that's wonderful," Madison said. "But I'm late for class already, so you'll have to tell me while we walk."

Madison started trotting down the hallway while Stuart and

Timothy struggled to keep up. "Slow down!"

"Can't do that," Madison said. "I'm late."

Stuart just could not keep up. He stopped, out of breath, and collapsed down to his knees. "We know who did it."

Madison stopped. "Why didn't you say something in the first place?"

Timothy stepped in between them. "I think it's a little presumptuous to say that we've found the culprit, but we have what amounts to an excellent suspect."

Stuart called out, still on his knees. "We finally have something to take to the police. Something real."

"No way," Madison said. I just talked with some idiot detective this morning. The police don't know anything. Tim has a more advanced lab than they do. No, we need to give them enough evidence to arrest this guy immediately. We need evidence."

"Great. Let's meet after school, and we'll go track this guy together." Stuart stood.

"Not a chance," Madison said. "This is too important to wait another minute. Give me the name. I'm going now."

"If you go, then I'm coming with you," Stuart said.

"Suit yourself," Madison said. "Hope you can keep up."

Timothy grabbed Stuart's arm. Stuart struggled to break free. "Are you crazy? You can't just leave school."

By the time Stuart had wrestled away from Timothy, Madison was halfway down the hallway and jogging down a flight of stairs. "Try to stop me. It's called being a friend, Tim. Try it sometime."

Stuart ran after her. "We'll have to get some supplies from the lab. Wait. Stop. Help!" Stuart stumbled as he clutched his side and disappeared down the stairs. "Charlie horse! You're too fast."

Timothy turned to see Mr. Reed glaring at him. "Where are those two going in such a rush?"

Timothy shrugged. "No idea."

Chapter 10
The Bug

The Gumshoes lab looked like a tornado had ripped through it. Stuart and Madison searched everywhere, flipping over chairs, rummaging through the pile of comic books, and—heaven forbid—moving Timothy's equipment to look into the crevices between the machines.

"Have you found it yet?" Stuart shouted from behind Timothy's desk.

"I don't even know what I'm looking for really, so no," Madison said from under the couch.

"It's a round, magnetic GPS tracker roughly the size of a nickel. There's a wireless microphone taped to the back. We'll use it to listen to Otis Howard's conversations and the GPS to track his movement. We had six of them before—well, let's just say some of us are forgetful about recovering them from cases."

"Yes, that would be you, Stuart," Timothy said as he walked into the room. "We've had a number of bugs destroyed by guilty parties, particularly when one of us hasn't been very astute in hiding them. You could've just asked for my help."

"I didn't think you'd leave school," Stuart said. "You've never missed a class. Not one in your entire life."

Timothy reached under his desk and pulled out a small, plastic box. "Yes, well some things are more important."

"Like friendship?" Stuart asked.

"Possibly."

"Maybe there's hope for you yet."

Timothy flipped open the box to reveal three microphones, with tracers attached, inside. "Don't be an idiot. I've got to make sure you don't destroy my equipment. I hid them for just such an occasion."

"A classmate's father being kidnapped?" Madison asked.

"No, one in which I can be the hero," Timothy said.

Stuart slapped Timothy on the back. "You're weird. Weird, but brilliant. Can you stay here and track the bug once we've placed it?"

"Of course," Timothy said. "It's what I'm best at."

Stuart snapped the plastic box closed and slid it into the side pocket of his backpack. "Great. Madison and I will head to the plant. With our bikes we should get there just about the time Otis gets to work."

Stuart held out his hand. "Thanks, buddy."

Timothy shook Stuart's hand before watching them run out the door.

***

Unlike the average scientific facility with a stuffy atmosphere and a sleek, contemporary design within a white-walled periphery, Thomas Pharmaceuticals had converted a two-story World War I munitions factory into a fifty-story behemoth. They had not only kept the brick façade but also moved the smokestacks onto the roof in order to pay homage to the town's roots. While its smokestacks no longer released hazardous chemicals, and its weapons assembly lines had long been removed, the structure still maintained the ominous look that reminded all passersby of both simpler, and more dangerous, times.

Mr. Thomas, the company's founder, wanted to retain authenticity—down to the wrought iron gate that encircled the entire facility. The company added only one modern amenity to the periphery of the building: a security post at the entrance. Security monitored incoming and outgoing traffic from the post—from the deliveries down to nosy detectives. And while the silver-haired, kindly security guard, Irv, did not scare many people with his doughy physique and severe sciatica, one call into the building summoned more than thirty security guards to his position in under fifteen seconds.

Madison and Stuart stopped their bikes in front of Thomas Pharmaceuticals and watched old Irv check every ID badge as the employees drove through the gate.

"How are we going to get inside?" Madison said.

Stuart opened his backpack and pulled out the paper bag containing his lunch. "Don't worry. I have a plan."

"Is it any good?"

"Unclear. Just follow me." Stuart pedaled his bike toward the security gate.

Madison followed behind. "Wait. You're going right up to him? I thought you had some sort of plan to climb up the bars."

"Are you kidding me?" Stuart said. "They must be fifteen feet high with big spikes on top. No, this is the only way."

Stuart stopped behind a black SUV. Irv looked down at his clipboard to check the license plate against a list of approved cars. "Mr. Johnson. You have a very nice day."

"Excuse me," Stuart said as the SUV drove onto the lot.

The unexpected noise caused Irv to jump out of his seat. As he noticed the unthreatening Stuart, he settled back down and waved another car toward him. "Yes, young man. I'm very busy. If you wouldn't mind moving along, I need to get back to work."

Stuart hopped off his bike and leaned it against the fence. He held up the paper bag toward Irv. "My father forgot his lunch. Mom told me to stop by on my way to school and drop it off."

"And what is your father's name?" Irv asked.

"His name——" Stuart inched closer to get a look at the clipboard. He blurted out the first name he saw.

"Fred Thomas."

"I highly doubt your father is the owner of the company, son," Irv said. "I think you need to move along. Head off to school."

Stuart puffed his chest out, offended. "How dare you, sir."

"Excuse me?" Irv said.

"What is your name?" Stuart demanded.

"I don't think——"

"My father will want to hear about this, and I want to be sure I know who he should fire. Now, you will tell me your name, sir."

"Well, I . . . I'm very sorry. It's just that I know he goes out to lunch, and he's never mentioned a son to me."

"Are you friends with my father?"

"I like to think we have a professional relationship."

"Have you ever been to our house for dinner?"

"Well, no."

"Has he ever taken you golfing or invited you onto his fishing boat?"

"No."

"Then how dare you presume to know the inner workings of his household. Now, our mom is trying to make him eat healthier, and in so doing, stop him from eating out every afternoon. In order to do that, she's had our housekeeper prepare his lunch: a healthy tofurkey sandwich with celery sticks and a fruit cup. Do you want him to die?"

"No," Irv said. "I love your father."

"Then, please, for the love of all things, allow me to give him his lunch!"

Irv blubbered like a child. Madison snickered under her breath, admiring Stuart.

Finally, his eyes made contact with Stuart. "Y-y-yes, sir."

Stuart gave a stern look before he grabbed his bike and walked through the gate. "You never told me your name, sir."

"Benson, sir. Irving Benson."

"I like you, Irv," Stuart said. "I'm going to tell my dad to keep an eye on you."

Irv's expression turned from sorrow to exhilaration as he

beamed with pride. "Really, sir? Oh, thank you, sir!"

"Don't mention it. Seriously. Ever. If you do, I'll know."

Madison and Stuart made their way into the parking lot. Once out of Benson's earshot, Madison whispered to Stuart. "I'm impressed. You got me thinking you were Fred's son for a second there."

"It's what I do," Stuart said. "Now we just have to figure out who Otis Howard is and which car is his. Shouldn't be that hard."

"Are you kidding me? Look at them all!" There were thousands of rows of cars; each row held hundreds of cars with almost identical colors, makes, and models.

Stuart pulled the walkie-talkie out of his backpack, crouching down behind a row of cars. "I'll call in the cavalry. Maybe Timothy can figure out the license plate. Meanwhile, we just have to wait."

Madison plopped herself down next to him. "This is not what I expected at all. Can't we just break all these windows or throw down some ninja moves? Anything else."

"Sorry it's not all excitement. Welcome to the tedious world of the stakeout."

***

The walkie-talkie crackled as Timothy sat in front of his computer. "All right. It'll take a few moments to procure that information. I will promptly return the information to you once it becomes available."

Timothy placed the walkie-talkie down and set Spike to work infiltrating the DMV database. Before he could open the browser window, his father screamed from the base of the tree. "Timothy. I received a communication from your school that you left before attending any classes. This is very disturbing, Timothy. I know you're inside. Lower the ladder right now, mister!"

Timothy continued to fiddle with his keyboard. "Fine then," his father continued, "I'm coming in. Prepare to be busted, mister!"

Stuart's voice came through the walkie-talkie. "Any word yet, Tim? We're so bored over here."

Timothy picked up the walkie-talkie. "Maintain radio silence. Code Fuchsia."

"What's Code Fuchsia? And what's that sound?"

Timothy heard it too. A slam reverberated against the tree house. He peered out the window to see his father climbing a ladder up to the tree house. "Wow, I can't believe that possibility never occurred to us before."

Timothy's only available option was to hide. He crawled under the desk, but his father would look there first. Then, he dove under the couch, but his gangly feet stuck out. He even sank into Stuart's pile of old clothes, but the stench caused him to gag after barely two seconds. Finally, he looked at the window opening. Madison had climbed up from the ground, so there must be a hold right outside the window.

Timothy climbed up onto the ledge and saw a branch outside the window. His intense fear of heights—a long-standing phobia that his father was well-acquainted with—would provide cover for his exit out onto the ledge.

"Don't look down. Don't look down. Don't look down." Timothy closed his eyes and grabbed onto the branch. "Keep. It. Together."

The door to Gumshoes headquarters opened as Timothy leaped onto the tree branch.

From the tree branch, Timothy could barely make out the top of his father's head, which ping-ponged haphazardly from one side of the room to the other.

After several minutes, Timothy heard his father say, "Well, I guess he's not here then. Where could that boy be?" Timothy's arms were burning and his grip was faltering; he wished his father would give up and leave quickly.

His father's phone rang. "Yes, sir. I understand, but I had to . . . Yes, sir. I'll be there right away." Timothy's father hung up his phone. "That boy is so lucky. He'll get his later on."

Timothy watched his father's head bob out of the tree

house. He let out a sigh of relief and then fought to make his way back into the tree house. Timothy sat down at his desk; soon, he was back into his rhythm.

Within seconds he had cracked the database, and Timothy navigated inside the system. Timothy pulled up Otis Howard's file and picked up his walkie-talkie.

"I found him," he said. "License plate GLS-9782. Do you see it?"

***

Stuart and Madison stood in front of a white luxury sedan with the license plate GLS-9782. Stuart clicked the walkie-talkie. "Got it. Thanks buddy."

Stuart stuffed the walkie-talkie back into his backpack. "All right. I'm going to place the tracer; you stay here and be the lookout."

"No way," Madison said. "I want to see what you do. This is my case, too."

"Mad——"

"It's my dad."

"Fine." Stuart pulled one of the bugs out and flipped it on. "All right, the tracer is easy. We just slap it on the bottom of the car like so." Stuart bent down, unclipped the microphone, and placed the tracer under the front bumper of the car. He flicked it on. "It's magnetic. Now we'll know exactly where he's going."

Stuart picked up the walkie-talkie. "Are you reading the signal, Tim?"

"Loud and clear. Signal is strong."

Stuart ambled around the car to the front passenger's side window with Madison behind him. "The bug is harder because, obviously, we have to get it into the car."

Stuart circled the car, looking at each window to see if one was open. Unfortunately, all the windows were sealed shut. "Crud. They usually leave a window at least slightly cracked." He turned to Madison. "Don't suppose you have a wire hanger on you?"

"Oh yeah," she said. "Let me just pull it out of my gigantic, everything purse."

As they bickered Stuart saw a tall and muscular man, dressed in a custom-tailored three-piece suit, exit the building and move toward the car. His taught skin belied his age, and his bald head shimmered in the morning light. He walked through the parking lot with not only determination but also the gait of a much younger man.

Stuart picked up the walkie-talkie. "Don't suppose you have any information on Otis from his license do you, Tim?"

"Hold one second," Timothy said.

"Don't really have any more time," Stuart said.

The walkie-talkie crackled. "Six feet, three inches tall. No hair color, so he must be bald, and driving glasses are mandatory in all instances. Why?"

"I think we're about to be found out." Stuart turned to Madison. "Run."

Stuart and Madison zigzagged through the cars as Otis unlocked the white sedan and stepped inside. The car backed out of the parking spot and turned the corner, out of sight.

"There goes that," Stuart said.

"Why don't we just go after him?" Madison said.

"Because he has a car and we have bikes."

"Right."

"Plus, I don't think we can get in here again. We could— no, it's too dangerous. But I have a plan."

"What? Tell me. I'll do anything."

"We go and place the bug in Otis's office, but it's way riskier."

"Let's do it."

"All right then."

Madison and Stuart walked toward the building entrance as the sun rose over the Thomas Pharmaceuticals complex.

Chapter 11
Break In

From the outside of Thomas Pharmaceuticals, one could never imagine the slick, glossy, egg-shell white veneer of the inside. The sleek floors clacked every time loafers or high heels stepped on them, and the futuristic design of the walls reflected as well as any mirror. In the center of the lobby against the far wall stood a high-gloss, circular reception desk, and seated in the middle of it was a jolly, plump receptionist. Along the wall, next to the reception desk, was a white door—the only entrance into the office corridor.

Several individuals in expensive suits sat on uncomfortable, white, plastic chairs to gain access through the door. Every few seconds they shifted positions, only to find the new position less comfortable than the last.

"Remember, I'm doing all the talking," Stuart said.

Madison rolled her eyes. "It's really boring being your sidekick sometimes. I can speak, too."

"I know. You just need some more training, young padawan."

"Really? All right, smart guy. Work your magic."

They approached the reception desk, listening to the receptionist greet each bustling employee passing through. Madison and Stuart stood patiently as she waved to a young scientist.

Five seconds went by, then ten, then twenty. Close to a minute passed without the receptionist noticing Stuart's and Madison's presence. Finally, Madison cleared her throat and the receptionist looked down at her. "Well hello, little lady. How may I help you today?"

Stuart looked over at Madison; she hesitated to continue. "Go ahead," he said. "Wow me."

Madison smiled as she turned back to the receptionist. "Yes, well, we're trying to give a package to somebody in a place. You know?"

"No. I'm sorry. I don't follow."

Madison froze, unable to think straight. Man, she thought, Stuart made this look so much easier. "It's just. Father. Lunch."

Madison threw her arms down to her side in frustration.

Stuart stepped up to take over. "What my painfully shy sister is trying to say is that we're trying to get our dad's lunch to him. We called up and he should be down any minute. Do you mind if we wait in your lobby?"

"Absolutely not. Please be my guest."

"Thank you, ma'am."

Stuart grabbed Madison's arm and gently pulled her across the room. They sat on the uncomfortable, white, plastic chairs to regroup. "What did we learn?"

Madison flopped down so hard on the unforgiving chairs that she nearly bruised her tailbone. "You make it look so easy."

"It's okay," Stuart said. "It took years of practice for me to be able to lie through my teeth like that. You'll get there." Stuart watched a pair of employees, dressed in long, white lab coats, slide their cards through a card reader and disappear into the secured office area. As the door closed, he noticed a bathroom on the opposite end of the hallway.

Stuart opened his lunch bag and pulled out a juice box. He tore off the straw and punctured it. "I'm really sorry about this, Madison."

"Excuse me?" she said.

Before she could form an eloquent protest, Stuart squirted juice all over Madison's pants. Madison jumped up and started wiping herself off before it stained. "Oh my—what did you—I can't believe you!"

Stuart dragged her back up to the receptionist. "I'm so sorry, but my sister had a little accident. Is there a bathroom around here?"

"The only bathroom is available to employees."

Stuart pointed to the stain on Madison's crotch. "I understand; believe me, all of these people waiting in your lobby are surefire hooligans. I can see it in their eyes. But look at us. We're kids. What's the worst we could do? Besides, if we don't set it soon, it'll be permanent."

Madison choked up. "I just bought these pants. They're the last thing my father——"

"You see how upset she is," Stuart said. "How can you deny that face?"

"Say no more." The receptionist pressed a button under the counter, and the door to the secured area kicked open.

"Thank you so much."

Stuart pushed Madison through the door as it swung shut behind them. He stood in astonishment. "That was brilliant. You're a natural!"

Madison wiped her tears away. "Thanks. But did you really have to destroy my favorite pair of pants?"

Stuart rummaged through his backpack and pulled out a

bottle of stain stick. He handed it to Madison. "Here. When you're as sloppy as I am, you need to be prepared. Go into the bathroom and take care of yourself. I'm going to get in touch with Timothy."

Madison disappeared into the women's bathroom. Stuart walked over to the company directory adorning the nearest wall as he pulled out his walkie-talkie. "Tim. Tim. We're in. Come in, Tim." Nothing but static. "Tim. Come on, buddy. Tim!"

Stuart put the walkie-talkie back. "These walls must be too thick to get a signal."

***

Back at the tree house, Timothy heard static coming from his walkie-talkie and picked it up. He made out only the garbled mumblings of every fifth word or so—nothing that could be construed as a complete sentence. "Hello. Stuart? Come in, Stuart."

Nothing. Just static. "Hmm. Must be out of range."

Just then he looked at the screen, and a look of terror contorted his face. The tracer on Otis's car showed him returning to the building. He was still a few miles out, but if Timothy didn't get a hold of Stuart, they were going to be caught.

"Oh no." Timothy flipped open his cell phone. "I know you don't like new technology Stuart, but I'm about to save your bacon yet again."

Timothy dialed Stuart's number and waited for it to ring. While waiting for an answer, he heard a faint ringing coming from the couch. He approached the noise, reached in between the cushions, and pulled out Stuart's cell phone. "Man," he said. "It's at times like this I wish I had learned Madison's number."

***

In order to move around Thomas Pharmaceuticals, one needed a keycard—that is what Stuart learned while he waited for Madison to finish in the bathroom. He checked out the elevator: not only did one need a keycard to enter but also an additional fingerprint scan was needed to gain access to specific floors. A keycard must also be swiped in order to enter the stairwell in front of which Stuart stood.

As Stuart waited for the stairwell door to open, Madison exited the bathroom and handed the stain stick back to him. She had blotted the stain into a large wet spot on her inner thigh. "It doesn't look like I peed myself, does it?"

Stuart looked down at the big wet spot on her pants. With every fiber of his being he tried to choke down his amusement, but spurts of laughter spouted forth.

"You know what? You suck!"

Stuart chortled. "I checked out the company directory.

Otis's office is on the tenth floor."

"Awesome. Let's go."

"There's a problem: the elevators only work with a keycard. So we either have to wait for an employee to use the elevator or——"

A whistling scientist walked out of the stairwell and disappeared around a corner. Before the door closed, Stuart stuck his foot inside and grabbed the handle. Madison looked in and saw stairs that seemed to extend up into the heavens. "You've got to be kidding," she said.

"Come on. You're young. You can take it, right?"

"I meant *you* specifically have to be kidding," Madison said. "I can climb ten flights of stairs with no problem, but you get winded walking between classes."

"I think I'll manage."

"All right. If you say so. Let's go."

Madison headed up the stairs with Stuart quick on her heels. After a few steps his pace became sluggish, and he grasped his side in pain.

***

Stuart lay on the landing between floors nine and ten, enjoying the cold of the concrete against his searing-hot flesh. Madison had been right: climbing the stairs had been too much for him. It had been intense and sweat-inducing, and now his shirt was soaked. Stuart was done; his body had given up on him, and he was gasping for air.

Madison, on the other hand, felt wonderful; she had barely broken a sweat and now sat on the stairs just above Stuart, eating the sandwich from his lunch.

"I told you," she said. "It's physically exhausting, and you're not in shape."

Stuart, still gasping, spoke hesitatingly. "I. Can. Do it."

Madison sucked down the last bite of the sandwich and wiped the crumbs off her pants. "Oh really? Let's go then. Come on. You're only a few steps away."

"Just give me a second."

Madison grabbed hold of his arm and dragged him up the stair, his shoulder whacking against each stair. *Whack!* "Ow." *Whack!* "Ow." *Whack!* "Ow. Quit it!"

"Fine." Madison released him and he fell down the stairs back onto the landing. "Otis will be back eventually, you know. If we don't get in and plant that bug, this whole thing will be in vain."

"Go ahead," he said. "I'm right behind you."

"All right," Madison said. "If you insist. But quit dawdling." Madison opened the door to the tenth floor and exited the stairwell.

***

The offices on the tenth floor were nothing special. By itself the tenth floor hardly looked like the Research Oversight division for a large pharmaceutical manufacturer. It looked much more like an insurance company. Every office was decorated with a single ficus plant that sat in the left corner behind a cheap, wooden desk and ergonomic chair.

Stuart exited the stairwell huffing and puffing. He held his left shoe in one hand, and his right pant leg was ripped at the knee. As he looked around, he noticed that not one person occupied an office on the entire floor. The eerie quiet haunted him for a moment until he saw a familiar figure gesture to him from the office next to the stairwell.

"Hey, over here!" Madison screamed. "About time!"

Stuart hobbled into Otis's office and found Madison rummaging through the stack of paper on Otis's desk. Stuart took a seat at the computer and looked at the message displayed across the monitor. "Password required."

"Yeah, I tried that already."

The caller ID lit up and the phone rang. "Don't worry," Madison said. "It's been doing that nonstop."

Stuart looked down and recognized the number on the caller ID. "Wait a minute. That's Timothy's phone!"

Stuart picked up the phone as Madison yanked it away from him. "What are you doing?"

"Give it to me!" Stuart said. They struggled for another couple of seconds before Stuart ripped the phone away and stuck the receiver up to his ear.

"You have to get out now," said a familiar voice on the other end of the line.

"Tim?" Stuart said.

"Listen to me," Tim said. "Otis's car pulled into the parking lot and stopped moving three minutes ago. He's going to be back in his office any second. You need to get out of there now! And bring me something with his fingerprints on it."

Stuart slammed the phone down and gulped loudly. "We have to go. He's coming."

"Wait," Madison said. "What?"

Stuart looked around for an appropriate spot to place his bug. Unable to find a suitable location on the desk, he turned to the ficus plant. He fumbled around in his pocket until he found the microphone. He hid the bug inside the soil.

"Come on, hurry up," Madison said.

The elevator dinged, and Otis and several of his coworkers stepped out of the elevator, chatting. The group circled together, outside the elevator, in what could only be described as an impromptu meeting of minds.

Stuart reached over Otis's desk and grabbed a chewed-up number-two pencil for Timothy. Stuart stuffed the pencil into his pocket. Madison grabbed his collar and dragged him toward the stairwell. "Now!" she said. She pulled Stuart into the stairwell. As the door closed, Otis turned toward his office.

"Whew," Madison said. "That was close."

A few seconds passed. Madison and Stuart stood shell-shocked when the door opened and a petite young woman, dressed in a business suit, popped her head in. "What, may I ask, are you doing up here sneaking around?"

Stuart's mind went blank. Luckily, Madison stepped in to save them. "We were just playing around. Our dad works up on thirteen, and it's so boring up there. Sorry to bother you."

The young woman eyeballed Madison warily for a moment before she smiled. "Don't worry about it. And I agree with you. Up on thirteen? Yawn fest."

The woman shut the door, and Stuart patted Madison on the back. "You're learning well, young Jedi. Great detective you might someday be."

"What a dork," Madison said.

Stuart agreed. "I know."

Madison jumped down onto the next landing. Stuart followed far behind, already huffing and puffing after only a couple of steps. "Wait . . . for me."

Chapter 12

Otis's House

The first bell rang, and a bleary-eyed Stuart disjointedly ambled down the hallway. He held out his arm to open the door to his classroom, but Madison grabbed hold of his shoulder and spun him around.

"Whoa, cowboy," she said. "Don't think you want to go there."

Stuart realized the door he had tried to open was not his classroom. In fact, it was the girls' bathroom—the site of his greatest humiliation. "One time may be forgivable, but twice you're a pervert," Madison said.

Stuart let out a huge yawn as he cracked his back. "Yeah. That would've been embarrassing."

"What's got you so tired?" Madison asked.

"The tapes," Stuart said. "I listened to them twice last night, just to make sure I didn't miss anything. I've officially taken pharmaceutical manufacturing off my list of future careers."

Timothy exited the boys' bathroom just in time to hear Stuart's last comment. "How could it ever be *on* your list of potential careers? You must be smart to attempt such a profession."

Stuart stretched his arms over his head to regain his energy. "Well, let me just say that I couldn't be happier not to be a genius then."

Madison turned to Timothy. "And where were you while your friend almost died of boredom? Shouldn't you have been listening, too?"

"I was convincing my father that a very important science exhibit at the Klimhoffer Museum was a more valuable use of my time than school," Timothy said.

"And he bought that?" Madison said.

"Bought it? He called in sick today to see it for himself. It's actually quite fantastic. I highly recommend it—I've been three times already."

Stuart laughed, which sent the blood rushing back into his brain. His cognitive function returned to normal, and he noticed that Madison cradled an enormous tri-fold poster under her right arm. "How did I miss that thing?" Stuart said. "It's huge!

What is it?"

Madison stepped in front of Stuart and Timothy and unfurled the poster. Along the top read the headline "Monthly Trends in News," but the letters of the headline were magazine clippings, all cut out individually and pasted together—like a ransom note. That same theme was instituted throughout the poster on every subheading and important conclusion. "Remember, I said that my journalism teacher makes us put together collages, which talk about trends in the news. Well, it's due today."

Stuart and Timothy perused the poster and eventually landed on the center image: a picture of Madison's father with the headline "Lawyer Lost." They looked up at Madison, who grinned through her sorrow. "I couldn't leave it out if I wanted an A."

The second bell rang, and Madison closed her poster. "I have to drop this off. Can we get together later and listen to those recordings?"

"Sure. Bring some caffeine because it's boooorrring!" Stuart said.

Madison chuckled. "You're so funny. I'll meet you after school and we'll go over to the tree house together, okay?"

Stuart grinned like an idiot. "Sure. Yeah. See you after school."

***

Stuart and Madison sat on the couch at Gumshoes headquarters. They listened, over a set of speakers, to Otis Howard talk about his day to friends, type on his computer, and dictate notes to subordinates. "Jenny, take this down. We need to decrease the zinc component to one point three milligrams per thousand. That should increase cost efficiency by four percent across the board."

Stuart rolled his eyes and slouched in his chair. "Nine hours straight listening to this. There's nothing here except the dullest man in history. But can we fast-forward through it? No, because you never know when he might say something relevant. This blows chunks."

Madison leaned in closely, trying to listen despite Stuart's complaints. "Shhh. I can't hear."

"Fine. I've had enough! I need a break. I'm going to see what Timothy's doing."

Stuart walked over to Timothy's workstation and watched him dust the pencil with powder under an ultraviolet light. "Find anything?"

Timothy picked up the pencil and used adhesive tape to pull off a partial fingerprint. "Outside of the fact that this man's mouth is full of disgusting bacteria, nothing substantial. Could you try to get something more disgusting next time? Like a stool sample."

"I'll try, buddy," Stuart said. "Anything for you."

Timothy sighed. "I've run three different partial fingerprints, pulled from this pencil against the police database and those I pulled from the crime scene, and found not a single point of commonality. Unfortunately, outside contaminants severely compromised the integrity of these prints. Perhaps if you stole his keyboard, it would have proven to be an easier comparison."

"How am I going to steal a keyboard without it being noticed?"

"I don't know. How do you do any of the things you do? Now, please, this is the last fingerprint on the pencil. I need complete silence."

"Really, aren't you just running the data through a computer?"

Timothy placed the adhesive tape onto his scanner and digitized the print into his computer. "Yes, but you're quite annoying and not very intelligent, so I was hoping that might shut you up."

Madison bolted out of her chair, screaming. "Guys, over here now!"

Timothy and Stuart rushed over to Madison. "I switched from the tape backup to the live feed, to see if anything more exciting was going on, and I heard this."

Madison cranked up the volume. "Yeah, yeah. The plan is going perfectly. No, I have everything in my basement. Nope. Doesn't suspect a thing. Yes. I'm going to set everything up today. After tonight, everything will be cleaned up . . . You know, you'd think the cleaning staff would do a better job watering this plant. Jenny, bring me a water bottle."

Stuart's eyes bugged out of his head. "Oh, no. This isn't good."

They heard Jenny respond to Otis. "Here you go, sir."

Stuart's eyes clenched shut. "This definitely isn't going to be good."

Water was poured onto the plant, which was followed by a hissing sound, then silence.

Stuart kicked the couch. "Crap!"

Madison turned up the volume, but no sound emitted. "What? What happened?"

"I think it's obvious," Timothy said. "Stuart planted the bug in the wrong place. What's rule number one, Stuart?"

"Not anywhere it can get wet. I'm sorry. I panicked. I was in a hurry. The plant wasn't even dying. It was fine."

"And now we're in the dark again," Timothy said. "We just wasted a whole day of work."

"Not to mention the monetary——"

"Wait," Madison said. "You mean we lost all communication? But that was it. We were just about to get the confession on tape."

"I don't know what you want us to do," Stuart said. "Unless you plan to break into his basement and find out what he's talking about, we're screwed."

A devious smile crept across Madison's face. "That's exactly what I plan on doing."

"You can't be serious," Timothy said.

Madison nodded.

"No," Stuart said. "We're not doing it. It's too dangerous."

Madison looked at him, doe-eyed. "It's my father. Besides, I could just go without you."

"All right, we'll go," Stuart said. "But the moment I sniff danger, we're out of there. Deal?"

She pumped her fist. "Yes!"

Madison pulled Stuart toward the door. He yelled back to Timothy. "Figure out where he lives and get back to me."

Timothy plopped down at his computer. "Clean that blind, sir. Sweep that rug, sir. When did I become his employee instead of his partner? Oh, look. I've already found the address. Now I guess I'll just sit here and wait while they have all the fun."

Timothy snatched up his walkie-talkie. "Stuart, I have the

address."

***

Otis Howard's house belied his status in life. A two-story Victorian fixer-upper, the tresses hung in disrepair over a poorly attended garden. The windows swung free of their hinges, and the doors desperately needed replacement.

Stuart and Madison hid their bikes in the brush next to Otis Howard's home. As they slunk down to consider the next move, Stuart noticed a small utility window in the lower left corner of the house hidden by a lifeless bush.

"Thought this place would be nicer, given where he works," Stuart said. "It would be lucky to survive a strong sneeze."

"That's really all you can think about at a time like this?" Madison said. "My dad's in there!"

"Right. And I think I have a plan of how to get inside."

Stuart ran to a utility window leading into the basement and pushed aside the bush. Madison followed closely behind. "Hold this," he said. He pushed hard on the window, grunting with all of his might. "These old utility windows are usually painted shut and forgotten. But if you push hard enough, they'll snap open."

"How do you know that?" Madison said.

"I saw it on TV," Stuart said.

Sure enough, with one more shove the window snapped and flipped up. Stuart's displaced force sent him tumbling through the tiny window into the basement.

Madison screamed. "Are you all right?"

"Yeah. I'm good."

"Do you see anything?"

"No. It's dark down here. All I can see is the light from the window. Swing your legs in, and I'll help you down."

Madison swung her legs through the tiny window. "I'm about to search through a killer's basement. I must be an idiot. Stuart, I think this was a bad ide—ya!" Stuart yanked hard and Madison fell into the house.

*****

Madison steadied herself against an old-fashioned washer while she adjusted to the darkness. "It stinks down here—like rotten eggs. Can you turn on a light?"

Stuart ran his fingers along the wall until he felt a switch. He flicked it up and down several times to no avail. "Must not be working."

"No problem," Madison said. "As if being in a basement in a possible kidnapper's house isn't freaky enough without having to investigate in complete darkness. Dad. Dad. Are you down here? *Dad!*"

Stuart moved into the center of the basement. His face brushed against something stringy, like a cobweb. "Ew. Ew. Ew! Spiders."

Madison, deftly avoiding Stuart's chaotically flailing arms, reached out and felt not a cobweb, but a string. She yanked it and the lights came on. "Chicken."

"Please. If it had touched your face, you would have freaked out, too."

"Uh huh."

Exposed plumbing and concrete floors added yet another dimension of imperfection to a home already in disrepair. All manner of tools, clothing, nonperishable food, and useless trinkets were strewn across the floor. Wood beams, full of dry rot, ran along the length of the basement and looked like they could collapse at any moment. But Stuart concentrated on one object lying in the corner. He tapped Madison's shoulder, too scared to speak.

"What is it? The boogie man?" Madison turned and came face to face with a huge, black bag, the size of a full-grown man, lying across the floor. It was zipped shut and bursting at the seam. Along the top it read CORONER in big, stenciled letters.

"Oh no," Madison squeaked.

Madison and Stuart inched closer to the bag, full of trepidation. They knelt down on opposite sides of it.

"I don't think I can do this," Madison said.

"We don't have to," Stuart said.

"Yes, we do. If we want the police to come, we have to know. Otherwise, it'll be gone by tomorrow."

Stuart slowly moved his hands toward the zipper. As his fingers grabbed onto the zipper, he heard the front door creak open.

Stuart grabbed his walkie-talkie. "Timothy. Has Otis moved?"

The walkie-talkie crackled. "No. His car's still in the parking lot. Why do you ask?"

"The front door just opened. Somebody's in the house."

"Then I suggest you hide!"

The footsteps creaked along the floorboard above. With each step the dry, rotted beams buckled. The steps moved closer and closer to the doorway and the unfinished wooden stairs that led up to them. Countless bags, stuffed tightly into an open storage space under the stairs, formed a perfect hiding spot. "Quick—under the stairs."

Stuart and Madison crammed themselves in between a pile of old workout equipment and three garbage bags full of smelly, old shoes. As they burrowed their way into years of forgotten memories, the footsteps descended the stairs.

Creak. *Thump.* Creak. *Thump.* Creak. *Thump.*

Nestled safely behind a lifetime of junk, Madison created a hole and peered out. She watched Otis walk into the basement. "Did I leave the dang light on again? I'd lose my mind if it wasn't attached."

Otis walked over toward the body bag. "My back's going to go out if I have to drag this thing down here again. Glad it'll all be over real soon."

"Thing?" Madison whispered. "*My dad's a thing to him!* I'm going to——"

Stuart pulled Madison back before she could lurch forward and attack. "Quiet. This guy's possibly a murderer. You don't——"

"Possibly? *Possibly?*" Madison whispered angrily. "What's that bag say to you?"

"We're not going get anywhere if we're dead too."

Madison folded her arms, defeated, and peered out of the hold. She watched Otis bend down and sling the bag over his shoulder. He grunted as he rose to his feet, then turned and walked toward the stairs.

He stopped. "I'm going to lose my mind, I swear. One of these days."

Changing course, he walked over to the light and pulled the string. Now in darkness, Stuart and Madison could only listen as Otis ascended the stairs.

Thump. Creak. *Thump.* Creak. *Thump.* Creak.

Otis exited out the back door, slamming it behind him.

Madison and Stuart sat in silence with only their labored breathing, and the drip of the nearby sink, to break the silence.

Chapter 13

Confronting Otis

Madison popped out of the pile and stumbled up the stairs after Otis. Stuart tried unsuccessfully to pull her back.

"Where are you going?" he asked.

"Where does it look like?" she said. "I'm following that bag."

"You're crazy. If that's your father, Otis will kill you, too."

"Stuart, if that's my dad, there's no way Otis is getting away with this. If I have to stop him myself, my dad's going to have justice."

Madison fumbled her way to the railing and up the

staircase. Stuart saw Madison's silhouette push the door open and creep out. He climbed out of his hiding place and followed her. "Can't we talk about this?"

He scurried across the floor and ran up the stairs. Madison screamed with every ounce of her being. The scream not only echoed through the basement door but also shook the basement. "STOP IT!"

***

Stuart burst out the back door. Madison stood at the bottom of the deck across from the unfinished garden. Otis, stunned, dropped the bag. Stuart watched as Madison closed in on Otis and the bag. "I'm not going to let you get away with this."

Otis backpedaled into the overgrown shrubbery. "Excuse me, little girl? Were you just in my house?"

"That's right, and we saw everything. We know what you did, and you're about to get arrested. We have all the evidence we need right here."

Otis stepped forward, offended by Madison's tone. "Listen, I don't know what you think I did——"

As he moved within range, Madison kicked him in the shin and sent Otis reeling to the ground. "I'm not going to be stopped."

Otis nursed his sore shin as Madison bent down next

to the black bag. She placed her hand on the zipper and closed her eyes. "Dad. I'm sorry we didn't get here sooner."

Madison unzipped the bag, eyes still clenched shut. She opened her eyes and gasped in horror. Quickly those gasps turned into mumbled confusion. She turned to Otis. "What is this? Where is my father?"

She charged Otis. Stuart stepped into the spot that she had vacated and kneeled down to examine the bag. Over his shoulder, he heard Madison scream. "Where is he?"

"I have no idea what you're talking about," Otis said.

"Yes you do. Sylvester Alberts. My father. Where is he?"

"I don't know."

"Liar!"

Madison punched Otis hard in the stomach. "Where *is* he?"

Otis coughed. "I don't know what you're talking about."

Madison grabbed Otis's shoulder and kneed him in the chest. She crumpled on top of him and smacked him repeatedly with all of her might. "Tell me. Tell me. Tell me!"

Madison sobbed uncontrollably as Otis tried to push her off, but her fury gave her the strength of ten men. "I'll kill you!" she screamed.

Stuart, meanwhile, dug his hand into the bag and pulled out a pair of gardening sheers. Confused, he opened the bag. There was no body inside; not even one of a small vole. Instead, he found gardening implements of every shape and size.

He turned and saw Madison wailing on Otis. He rushed over and pulled Madison off him. "Madison. Stop!"

"No! He killed my dad. He did it. I know he did." Madison tried to get in a final flurry of kicks before Stuart pulled her away. Madison struggled and wriggled as hard as she could, but eventually she resigned herself and collapsed into a heap, crying and weeping uncontrollably on the ground.

"I'm very sorry about that. Her father is missing and we thought——"

Otis stood and wiped himself off. "You what—thought I kidnapped and killed him? What could possibly make you think that?"

"There was a file in her father's office. A red file. You made death threats against him. You work at Thomas Pharmaceuticals making chloroform, which was used to knock him out."

Otis shook his head. "I'll admit that evidence doesn't show me in a good light, but what you don't know is that we finally agreed to a settlement of my wife's case, and she's getting the treatment she needs."

"You said what in the where now?" Stuart said.

"My wife got very sick while working on a chemical compound for Thomas called J47S. While I continued to work for Thomas, my wife couldn't work anymore. We filed suit after Thomas refused to consider her claim a job-related injury. Mr. Alberts represented the company. I couldn't believe the company I had dedicated my life to would just watch my wife wither away. I was angry. Now I'm ashamed I sent those letters, but what else was I going to do? I had to get through to him somehow."

Tears formed in Otis's eyes. "She's my life. I can't go on without her."

Madison collected herself. "You're not helping your case."

"Let him finish," Stuart said.

"Thank you," Otis said. "Last week we had a breakthrough. Mr. Alberts called and told me the company had a change of heart. They agreed to settle, pay all of our back medical expenses, and give my wife the care she needs. So you see I love Mr. Alberts; he gave me my wife back."

"But we heard you talk about your master plan and

how it was all coming together," Stuart said.

"How did you——? My wife comes home this weekend, after being stuck in a hospital bed for six months. She loves nature, but even after coming home, she won't have the energy to do much more than walk outside and enjoy the garden. So I rented a pickup with one hundred different types of flowers so she can have something pretty to look at while she recuperates."

"Wow, I feel foolish," Stuart said. "Maybe we should've just asked you, huh?"

Otis reached into his coat pocket and pulled out a handkerchief. He walked over to Madison and handed it to her. "Here. Your father is a good man."

Madison took the handkerchief and blew her nose. "Thank you. I'm sorry—about everything."

Otis smiled and patted her on the head. "I understand more than you know. Thinking someone you love is in trouble tends to make you a little irrational."

As Otis and Madison shared a tender moment, Stuart heard the unmistakable sound of police sirens drawing near. "Um, did somebody call the police?"

Five police cars swarmed the street. Police officers scattered from their cars and took defensive positions around the home's perimeter. As the officers formed rank,

Stuart noticed several of Otis's neighbors gathering on their decks with looks of concern on their faces. An elderly woman stared at them from her perch in her bedroom. She held a cordless phone and grinned in silent admission.

Stuart gulped loudly. "Oh no. My dad!"

***

The East Willow Police Station was quite small and rustic in comparison to those in the surrounding cities and towns. Patrolmen and officers bumped elbows as they shared cramped desk space.

As the senior-ranking detective, Josiah had managed to secure an office at the furthest corner of the building, away from the hustle and bustle. Madison and Stuart occupied a corner bench as they stared at the ground in penance.

Madison's arms curled into themselves and her brow furrowed while Stuart's legs kicked in the wind. Every once in a while, a sigh would break the silence as they waited for Josiah to return and dole out their punishment.

Stuart awkwardly tried to break the silence. "So——"

"I can't believe your father is the same detective who is in charge of my father's case. Do you know how much I hate him?"

"I'm sorry."

"Not to mention you've been completely wrong about everything. You caused me to beat up an innocent guy. He was trying to do something nice for his wife. I can't believe you."

"It's not only my——"

"What? It's not your fault? You're saying *I'm* partially to blame? I can't believe you! You're the expert. I trusted you, and you betrayed me!"

"I just——"

"I don't want to talk about it. Let's just sit in silence."

"Okay."

Stuart opened his mouth to speak, but thought better of it. He looked down at his feet, consigned to his sorrow.

The silence built to a crescendo just as the door burst open, and Josiah stormed in. He threw a thick case file on his desk and paced wildly, unable to contain his fury. "I can't believe the two of you. If I read this case file correctly, you snuck into an office building, planted an illegal wiretap, trespassed, broke into someone's home, and assaulted a man with a gravely ill spouse. That about sum it up?"

Madison responded as Stuart sat contrite. "Yes, sir."

"You could be arrested for this. You could go to juvenile hall. Luckily, the man you harassed isn't filing charges."

Josiah pointed his bulbous finger at Stuart. "You are in a lot of trouble, mister. You've led this poor girl around on some wild goose chase and withheld evidence on a kidnapping investigation. What were you thinking?

Stuart bumbled through a clever excuse before giving up. "I . . . I wasn't, sir."

"No, you sure weren't." Josiah finished his tirade. "I'm glad you're both okay. Madison, I've already informed your grandmother that I will be taking you home. Come on. Let's go."

Madison stood and hurried out the door with a sullen Stuart following behind her. Watching Madison's rejection of Stuart, Josiah wanted to comfort his son, but did not know how. All he could do was give him a hard shove out the door. Picking up his fedora from the coatrack, he threw on his coat and closed the door behind him.

***

Josiah's unmarked police car had been fitted with every gadget a sleuth could want, from an information hub that tracked criminal records to bulletproof glass that separated him from criminals in the back seat. Unfortunately for him, those criminals currently happened to be his son and a naïve schoolmate.

Josiah parked the car and exited the vehicle. "Stuart,

you wait here while I walk Miss Alberts to her front door."
He closed the door. Stuart watched from the backseat as
Madison walked past her grandmother and into the house.
Josiah tipped his fedora and walked back to the car.

Once in the driver's seat, Josiah started the car and
drove away in silence. He snuck a stern glance through the
rearview mirror. Stuart locked eyes with his father and
wondered what horrible punishment he would have to
endure, and if there was even an iota of a chance that he
would ever be forgiven for his actions.

"You know," his father said, "I was in middle school
once, too. There was a girl, Theresa Williams. Man, I was
over the moon for her. Every day I would stand by her
locker and try to get a whiff of her hair. One day I gathered
up just enough nerve to ask her out. I walked up to her and
cleared my throat, but nothing came out. I stood there like
an idiot. Everybody pointed and laughed. I was humiliated."

Stuart had perked up. "What happened?"

"I ran away. Never talked to her again."

"Oh," Stuart responded, dejected. "Great story."

"My point, son, is that I always regretted it. You know,
not trying. Not going the distance to impress her and make
her aware of my existence. What I'm trying to say is that
you made a fool out of yourself today, but you don't have

to quit trying. You see my point, son?"

Stuart glared at his father. "No."

Josiah sighed. He was obviously no better at connecting with his son than with his wife. He resigned himself to driving in silence, listening to the whisper of the road.

Chapter 14

Amends

The next morning, Stuart hopped down the stairs and into the kitchen. He saw his parents locked in a heated conversation. "You should be nicer to him," his mother said. "He's just a boy!"

"And you shouldn't coddle him," his father said. "If I told you the stuff he's done, your head would explode."

"He's not a criminal. He's just trying to do some good in the world, like you."

Stuart's father looked over and saw Stuart enter the kitchen. His demeanor changed.

Stuart's mother stuffed her anger deep into the recesses of her face, slapped on a smile, and shuffled to the sink to clean the dishes.

"Mornin' sport. Your mother and I——"

"We were just talking," she interrupted. Two pieces of toast popped out of the toaster. She smiled. "Sit down. I made breakfast."

Stuart's eyes bounced back and forth between them. They were trying to look like the perfect couple in front of him, and his appetite vanished.

"No thanks. I'm not hungry." Stuart grabbed his book bag from the kitchen counter and ran out the back door.

Josiah watched him go and shook his head. "This is your fault."

Julie looked back at him with scorn and venom in her eyes. "I hope you burn your mouth on breakfast."

***

Stuart's stomach grumbled as he walked through the school hallway with Timothy. "I can't believe I didn't eat breakfast. I'm so hungry."

"Yes, the acids are eroding the lining of your stomach as we speak," Timothy said. "You should really head to the cafeteria and remedy your condition."

"I might as well eat cardboard," Stuart said.

"Both are quite unpleasant scenarios, but the latter a tad less so than starving to death."

Stuart grabbed his stomach in pain. "I can't go on like this. Fine, I'll eat the crummy cafeteria breakfast."

***

Stuart entered the cafeteria and saw Madison standing with Brad. She brushed a stray hair out of her face and laughed at one of his inappropriate jokes.

"Let's just go," Stuart said. "I can't look at her, Tim."

"Well, in all fairness your constant devotion to her made me feel slightly inadequate as your friend," Timothy said.

Stuart patted Timothy on the back. "I didn't know you had feelings, Tim."

"Me either."

Madison glanced at Stuart from the corner of her eye, and her jovial attitude devolved into a rage-filled scowl.

"This is uncomfortable," Stuart said.

Madison whispered something into Brad's ear. Immediately, Brad stood and escorted Madison toward the exit. As he passed, Brad slammed his shoulder against Stuart's. Stuart spun one hundred and eighty degrees and fell to the ground.

Stuart shouted at Madison. "You know we did our best to help you. You're just angry, and you're taking it out on us."

Madison stomped back toward Stuart. "No. I'm not taking it out on both of you. After all, Timothy's not to blame. You are.

He's just your lackey."

"Me?" Timothy said, flustered by the accusation.

"He just analyzes the data you give him," Madison said.

Timothy popped in between them. "I do a right bit more than that if you don't mind."

Stuart looked through Timothy as if he were a glass wall. "What do you want from me, Madison? I'll do anything."

"Just leave me alone." Madison turned and walked out of the cafeteria.

After she'd left, Chet strutted up to Stuart and Timothy. He cracked his knuckles and smiled. "Looks like you ain't got protectors no more, nerds."

Stuart tried to run. But Chet's strength was matched by his quickness. Before Stuart took a single stride away, Chet grabbed him by his underwear and pulled the waistband over Stuart's head, lodging it uncomfortably in the crack of his butt. "ATOMIC WEDGIE!" The cafeteria cackled in approval.

Stuart collapsed on the ground and Chet turned his attention to Timothy. Timothy backed away slowly so as not to aggravate the brooding beast. "Now, I think we can be civil about this. After all, I've not wronged you in any way."

Chet grabbed him by the shoulders. "That's not how it works, geek. You upset the balance of power, and now you'll pay."

Chet kneed Timothy straight between the legs. Timothy buckled under the intense pain.

"Remember that," Chet said as he high-fived a couple of his bully amigos.

Chet and his posse walked out of the cafeteria. Stuart rolled over toward Timothy. "We have to get back on Madison's good side. I can't live through this again. Not again."

"I wholeheartedly agree. But first, I must writhe in pain for the next several hours."

"I'm right there with you, buddy. After school then."

***

Stuart and Timothy walked into Mr. Alberts's office after school. Lou Lou Belle, as always, sat behind her desk. She fielded a myriad of questions from countless concerned clients with the ease and grace of a ballet dancer. The way the phones practically flew off their handles, Stuart would have thought Madison's father was hard at work in his office.

"Alberts and Mitchell, please hold. Alberts and Mitchell, please hold. Alberts and Mitchell, please hold. Alberts and Mitchell, thank you for holding. How may we help you?"

Timothy and Stuart walked up to the reception desk and waited for Lou Lou Belle to acknowledge their presence. Finally, she hung up the phone and smiled at them. "What can I do for you boys?"

"Do you remember me?" Stuart said. "I was here with Madison a couple of days ago."

"Of course," Lou Lou Belle said. "Why, you're her little bodyguard."

"Technically, he's more like a sentry," Timothy said.

Stuart shook his head. "Well, it seems like I left something very valuable inside the office, and I need to get it back."

Lou Lou leaned toward them. "Normally, I'd say it's a lost cause because our cleaning people are so darn top-notch, but since the police forbade us from lifting a finger to disturb any evidence, those sweet, little old ladies haven't been allowed in for days. I say go for it."

Timothy, confused, could not help but ask a follow-up question. "Excuse me, but if they're not allowed to disturb the crime scene, then why are you letting us into his office to do just that?"

Lou Lou Belle looked at him, confused and baffled for a moment. "I don't understand the question. Now, if you'll excuse me." She picked up the phone as Stuart and Timothy made their way into the office.

***

The door to the office closed and they began to snoop around. "We're looking for any proof someone had it out for Madison's dad," Stuart said.

"I'm not quite sure I understand," Timothy said. "Since we have all of the red files, why not just look through them?"

"We did that before and got squat," Stuart said. "There has to be something else."

Stuart made his way over to Mr. Alberts's desk. After Stuart looked through the pencil cup and in-box, he picked up the picture of Madison and her father fishing. She must have forgotten this last time, he thought to himself. For the first time, Stuart saw how happy Madison had been with her father—and the radiance she had exuded before he was taken away from her. Stuart wished that, just once, his father would illicit that sort of joy from him.

As he cradled the picture in his hands, he felt something pop, as if a piece of paper had been hastily wedged inside. Stuart flipped the latches that held the frame together and carefully removed the back. A folded-up piece of paper was crammed behind the photograph. Stuart unfurled it. The top of the document read "Agreement to Dissolve the Partnership between Sylvester Alberts and Peter Mitchell." Stuart flipped through to the final page of the document and noticed that the only signature was that of Mr. Alberts. "Tim, I think I found the smoking gun."

Timothy made his way across the room as the door flung open. A sinewy figure, cloaked in shadow, stood in the doorway. The figure stepped into the light. It was Madison!

"What are you two idiots doing here?" she said.

Stuart smirked at her. "I think we found something that might interest you."

***

Stuart, Madison, and Lou Lou Belle crowded around Mr. Alberts's computer while Timothy attempted to hack the files on the computer. Lou Lou Belle bit her lip. "I don't like this one bit. Mr. Alberts's clients are going to be really unhappy if they find out you were snooping through their private records."

Madison rubbed Lou Lou's back. "I know you don't like it Lou Lou, but if it leads to my father, then it'll all be worth it."

"I know, I know," Lou Lou said. "You've made it all very clear."

Timothy broke through the heavily encrypted firewall with Spike's help. "We're in. Now, let's see what we can find."

He opened the e-mail. As he searched past the thousands of client e-mails received since his disappearance, Timothy found the last e-mail to which Madison's father had responded.

The e-mail was marked Urgent. The subject line read "Earning Projections," and the body of the e-mail consisted of an attachment, which opened into a spreadsheet. Assuming the partnership disbanded, Mr. Mitchell's spreadsheet laid out the expected earnings of each of the partners over the next twenty years in painstaking detail.

"This is amazing," Timothy said. "Apparently, this partnership is worth two million dollars annually. However, if they dissolve the partnership, they would be lucky to make three hundred thousand dollars a year combined."

The squeaky wheel of Stuart's brain pieced the puzzle together. "No wonder Mr. Mitchell didn't sign the document. It's career suicide."

"Where is Mr. Mitchell now?" Madison asked Lou Lou Belle.

Lou Lou Belle thought for a moment. "I don't know. He keeps his own schedule these days. I could always call and let you know when I see him——"

Madison ran toward the door. "No time. Come on, guys. We'll check his house first. Maybe we'll get lucky."

"Does that mean we're friends again?" Stuart said.

"Quit asking dumb questions and hurry up." Madison disappeared from view.

"That wasn't much of an answer, was it, Tim?" Stuart said.

Timothy walked out the door with Stuart. "No, Stuart. It most certainly wasn't. But on the plus side, she doesn't seem to hate you at the present moment."

"True that, buddy."

***

Mr. Mitchell's house was not as palatial as Mr. Alberts's, but the location was nevertheless fabulous. The house looked out over East Willow Lake. Two-thirds of the house jutted out beyond rolling hills, supported by metal stilts to prevent it from sliding into the water below.

Madison opened the door to Mr. Mitchell's house and the three of them filed inside. Madison stepped down the three stairs that let into the main living area and onto the shag carpet. "It's lucky I feed his plants while he's away so I have a key to his house."

Stuart flipped on the lights. The entire house was in disarray. Much like Madison's house, it looked like a bullet train had ripped through one side and out the other.

Madison noticed the empty wall where a large, exotic fish tank had once been. Now, all that remained was shattered glass and dead fish strewn across the floor. Her shoe squished on the soaked carpet.

"He loved this fish tank," Madison said. "My dad said it was the only thing he cared about more than money. Some of these fish cost three thousand dollars."

"Are you kidding me?" Stuart said. "My mom's car didn't cost three grand."

As they made their way around the room, they heard a faint moaning coming from underneath the overturned coffee table.

"I don't like the sound of that," Timothy said.

Timothy and Stuart each grabbed a side and heaved the coffee table away, revealing a badly beaten, barely conscious Mr. Mitchell clinging to life.

"AAAAAHHHHHHHHHHHHHHH!" Madison let out a blood-curdling scream as Timothy and Stuart held onto each other, terrified.

Chapter 15

The Project

Josiah fumed at the top of his lungs, staring at Stuart, Madison, and Timothy.

"I can't believe how stupid you three are. Do you know I could arrest you for tampering with a crime scene?"

"I——" Stuart tried to interject.

"Do you three want to go to jail?" Josiah boomed.

"No, sir," they said in unison.

As Josiah slammed his fist down, paperwork from cluttered case files that had been strewn about his desk flew into the air and floated gently onto the floor.

Madison raised her hand. "How is Mr. Mitchell?"

Josiah looked over at her. "He's in a coma at County General. We have a police guard stationed outside his room twenty-four hours a day. Nobody goes in or out except the medical staff. Not family, not friends, and definitely not snoopy children. So don't even think about it."

Madison breathed a sigh of relief. "Is he going to be all right?"

"We don't know," Josiah said. "And don't think for a second that finding Mr. Mitchell gets you off the hook . . . I can't believe this. You two were just in here. And now you've brought poor Timothy into your delinquency."

Josiah marched up to his son and stuck one of his big, knobby fingers in his face. "You're on a slippery slope, pal. Your mother wanted me to take it easy on you, but I can see this has gone too far. I'm tearing down your little tree house in the morning. Kiss the Gumshoes Detective Agency good-bye."

Timothy raised his hand. "But, sir, I believe my father built that house, and it's only with his approval that you can dismember it."

Josiah turned a puzzled eye to Timothy. "His approval? This was his idea! You've skipped school and been hauled down to the police station; he just didn't think that would look good on your college transcript."

Josiah turned his attention back to Stuart. "And you? You are a disappointment. Is there anything you have to say for yourself?"

Stuart's eyes rose to meet his father's gaze. "Just one question, Dad."

"What is it? Come on, spit it out."

"Is that the case file on your desk?" Stuart asked.

Smoke nearly steamed out of Josiah's ears. "Mister, you are about one word away from being knocked into the next century."

As Josiah gritted his teeth in a veiled attempt to quell his anger, a young patrolman burst into the office. "Detective. We need you."

"Can't you see I'm talking to my son?"

"I'm sorry, sir, but they need you immediately in the conference room. I was told not to come back unless I brought you with me."

Josiah sighed. "Fine. You three stay put. I'm taking a mental picture, and if I find one piece of paper out of place on my desk, well, you don't want to know what will develop."

Josiah and the patrolman walked down the hall toward the conference room. Once they turned and were out of sight, Stuart hopped up and rummaged through the papers on his father's desk.

Madison rose to stop him. "Are you crazy? Your dad's going to kill you!"

"Yeah, it's highly unlikely this can end in a positive

outcome," Timothy said.

"Relax guys," Stuart said. "Look, he's only mad because he thinks we're interfering in the case. But if we find something, how can he be mad at that?"

"That's stupid, Stuart," Madison said. "He's mad because you're putting yourself in harm's way."

Timothy nodded. "Correct, Madison. Not to mention that you're breaking the law, Stuart."

Stuart smirked as he examined a single sheet of paper. "Relax, guys. Sometimes you've got to break the law to enforce the law. Take a look at this."

Stuart held up the paper to them. It was a ransom note that had been glued together from different pages from countless different magazines.

Timothy read the note aloud as he tried to make sense of it in his head. "I have the lawyer. No funny business. One hundred grand by tomorrow." Timothy shook his head. "That doesn't make any sense. There are no further instructions."

Stuart smiled. "I know. The kidnapper's trying to throw the police off the trail."

"How do you figure?" Madison said.

"If the kidnapper were interested in money, then he would have specified the time and place of drop-off. Not to mention the idea of writing a ransom note with cut-out magazine clippings is antiquated and gimmicky. No, this guy was looking to put on a show. This isn't about money; it's about something else."

"What?" Madison said.

"I don't know, but something bugs me," Stuart said. He pointed to the green, uppercase L that started the word *Lawyer*. "I recognize this letter. I've seen it somewhere before."

Madison bent closer to examine it. "Where?"

"In that magazine I read at your dad's house, and again on the poster presentation you brought in."

Timothy squinted and pressed his glasses closer to his nose. "That's highly implausible. It looks like a green L to me."

Stuart dropped the note back onto the desk and rushed toward the door. "Trust me. Come on. I have to test a theory."

Timothy and Madison both replied vehemently. "No way!"

Stuart turned back to them. "You two are more alike that you realize. You're both wet blankets. Now, if you want to solve this case, you need to follow me. Now."

Stuart ducked down and ran out of his father's office toward the exit. Timothy and Madison looked at each other for a long moment before shrugging their shoulders and following Stuart out the door. As they rounded the corner toward the exit, Josiah walked back into his office.

"STUART!" he yelled.

***

Inside Gumshoes headquarters, Timothy typed while Madison and Stuart paced back and forth. "Find anything yet?" Stuart said.

The printer heated up—Timothy had finished his search—and Stuart ran over to it to pick up the page as it printed out. "*Better Landscaping* isn't sold in any East Willow stores. The closest shipment is fifty miles away. But there are thirty people who subscribe to *Better Gardening* in East Willow. I'll bet you anything ninety-nine percent of them have Mr. Reed for journalism."

A second page printed, and Madison snatched it. "Why are you printing out criminal records for Mr. Reed?"

Stuart grabbed the document and looked it over. "Mr. Reed hit a student with his car last year and was suspended from teaching for the rest of the year. He had to move school districts. And look at this. Who was the lawyer for the school district in the wrongful termination case he lost? Your father."

"They why wasn't his case in my father's red files?" Madison said.

"He must have never submitted a death threat," Timothy said. "That doesn't mean he didn't hold a grudge, though."

Stuart pulled another printed page from the printer tray. "His wife filed for divorce two months after he had lost that case. Well there's no doubt he had a motive. And you told me he'd come back to school after running errands on the day your father was taken, which gives him opportunity."

As the trio huddled around to analyze the data, they heard Stuart's father yell up to them. "That's it, kids. It's over."

Stuart poked his head out the window.

His father was holding a ladder, with Timothy's father close at his heels. "You can't run, Timothy. We have you. Stay put."

Stuart stepped onto the ledge of the nearest window. "Timothy, it's time to activate protocol Charlie."

The ladder slammed down on the entrance to the tree house. "I hate protocol Charlie," Timothy said.

"What's protocol Charlie?" Madison asked.

Stuart tugged on the zip line. "This is protocol Charlie."

Madison looked at the zip line cable. "Awesome."

"It's now or never," Stuart said.

Madison climbed onto the ledge and grabbed onto the cable. She pushed herself off and screamed with glee all the way down.

Stuart beckoned to Timothy. "Come on, man."

Stuart helped Timothy onto the ledge. Timothy grabbed onto the zip line and inched his way toward the edge. "Science, please save me." He pushed himself off and slid down.

Josiah climbed to the top of the ladder and rushed toward

Stuart. "Get over here this minute!"

Stuart stuffed the printout into his shirt as he leaped onto the zip line. "Sorry, Dad."

Josiah watched his son roll onto the ground and disappear with his friends into the night.

***

Madison, Stuart, and Timothy walked through the dark school hallway. The moonlight accentuated and glistened off the lockers, adding just the perfect amount of light to recognize the outlines of the lockers and classroom doors, but nothing smaller.

Madison whacked herself on the corner of a locker. "We should've brought flashlights."

"Well, the next time *you're* saving *my* bacon, make sure to have them handy," Stuart said.

"I'm just saying I don't understand what we're doing here."

Timothy sidestepped a janitorial bucket. "It's fairly logical in my opinion, but I'll cede to Stuart."

"Here's the deal," Stuart said. "Your poster had that exact letter L carved out of it. If we break into Mr. Reed's room and the letter is gone, we'll know he's the guy."

Madison stopped in her tracks. "That doesn't make any sense. What if he just bought another issue or what if the letter fell off somewhere else? It's not like glue's infallible."

"Oh yeah?" Stuart said. "Well, I'm sure there are a lot of subscribers to that magazine who also have a huge grudge against your father."

"It could happen," Madison said.

They reached Mr. Reed's classroom. Stuart pressed the handle and the door swung open. "He didn't lock his door. I like a trustworthy sucker."

Madison followed Stuart and Timothy inside. "And you don't think that's a little weird for a kidnapper?"

Timothy flipped the switch and the lights flickered on. The poster boards were lined up along the window on the opposite wall. They walked up to Madison's poster. Sure enough, the exact same letter L was missing that had been on the ransom note.

Stuart beamed. "I told you."

Timothy scanned the row of posters. "That's not all."

They looked at the poster next to Madison's. Two letters had been removed. The poster on the opposite side of Madison's was missing three letters. In fact, every poster in the room had at least one letter missing. They searched along the floor and found none of the missing letters.

"What now?" Madison asked.

"We let my dad know," Stuart said. "No more secrets."

"But he's after you," Timothy said. "You'll never be able to get through to him."

"Leave that to me," Stuart said. "Meet me at Mr. Reed's house in an hour and bring some popcorn. It's going to be quite a show."

***

Josiah, tired and weary, walked into his office and slumped down in his chair. On his desk was a red folder that had not been there earlier. He opened it up and found not only all the information Stuart had gleaned about Mr. Reed but also pictures of the posters with missing letters. Josiah smiled before he closed the folder and screamed into the station. "Get me a judge!"

Chapter 16

Revelations

Mr. Reed's home sat on a hill on the outskirts of town, a few blocks from the reservoir on Unger Street. While not older or smaller than other neighborhoods, the town residents looked down on homes close to the reservoir as refuges for outcasts and lowlifes. It was not an unwarranted comparison. Still, it was one of the few affordable homes for a single father of a young daughter. Price was even more important to a teacher who had been forced to take a tremendous pay cut by starting over in a new town.

The home itself was quaint. It was not as large as Stuart's home, but it was not a rambler or duplex, either. A two-story, red-shuttered colonial, the roof jutted out over the front door, which was supported by four thick, white-washed wooden posts.

Timothy and Madison sat in the bushes outside of Mr. Reed's house. The lights from police cruisers twenty-deep lit up the night as patrolmen and detectives filed in and out. Mr. Reed stood outside—scared, confused, and holding his doe-eyed, four-year-old daughter—conversing with Josiah.

"I thought I would get more enjoyment out of this," Madison said.

"There is no satisfaction in revenge if it doesn't help solve the initial crime," Timothy said. "Once you reunite with your father, you will feel elated."

"You know, we're not so different, Timothy," Madison said.

"I must admit," Timothy said, "over the past few days I've realized that we have more in common than not. That must be why Stuart likes you so much."

Madison blushed. "Really?"

"Yes. You must remind him of me. It's the only conclusion that makes sense as to why he's abandoned me." Timothy's head dropped, caught off guard by his emotions.

"He hasn't abandoned you," Madison said. "We would have never been here without your great work. Besides, he can get a little annoying at times. Count yourself lucky you don't have to hang out with him every day. I'll be more than happy to give him back once this is over."

"You're trying to comfort me. It has worked. Thank you." As Timothy smiled and nodded at her in appreciation, they heard rustling in the bushes. Startled, they turned around. Stuart wedged himself between them. "What did I miss?"

"Oh, nothing." Madison smirked and turned her attention back to the house. The detective laughed and shook Mr. Reed's hand before he walked to his car. "What are they doing? This guy kidnapped my father. Why are they leaving? No. No. NO!"

Madison tried to stand, but Stuart dragged her back down to the ground. "Listen, if we go out there now, the police will stop us from talking to him on our own. We have to wait until the coast is clear, and then we'll get in there. I promise."

Madison unhappily settled herself, watching the police pack up and drive away.

***

Half an hour later, the last police car vacated Mr. Reed's driveway. The moment it was out of sight Madison stood and made a beeline for the house. "Now it's time. I'm going."

"Wait for us," Stuart said.

Madison ran up the front stoop and banged on the door. Stuart and Timothy, huffing and puffing, closed the gap between them. From inside they heard the muffled sounds of

Mr. Reed running down the stairs. "Come on. What do you want now? Haven't you disturbed my daughter's sleep enough?"

Mr. Reed flung open the door in anger, but that anger quickly turned to confusion when he saw the Gumshoes. "Madison, Timothy, Stuart? What are you doing here?"

Madison took an uninvited step into Mr. Reed's house. "Where is he, Mr. Reed?"

"Where is who?" Mr. Reed said.

"You know who! My father! Where is my father?"

"Listen, I don't know what you heard, but the police were wrong. I don't—"

Madison stomped on the hard foyer floor. "I know what I saw. I know what I heard. I know. I know. I KNOW!"

Mr. Reed grabbed Madison's shoulders, trying to calm her down. "What are you talking about? I've had a day, and this is about all I can take!"

Stuart pulled Mr. Reed off Madison and stepped between them. "We know about your case, and your grudge against Mr. Alberts. We saw the posters in your classroom. Letters were ripped off that corresponded to a ransom note the police received."

"What ransom note?" Mr. Reed said.

"The one you wrote demanding payment for the return of

Mr. Alberts," Timothy said.

Mr. Reed rubbed his temples. "That doesn't make any sense."

"Actually, it makes perfect sense," Timothy said. "You hit a student with your car; soon after, your wife left you. I found documentation to prove it. You were forced to give up your life and move to a new town. It's understandable that you would be angry with Mr. Alberts."

"Why?"

"Because he defended the school district in your wrongful termination case," Madison blurted out.

Mr. Reed slammed his fist against the wall in protest, causing the entire house to shake and rumble. "That's enough. Now, I loved my wife and I was furious at the school district; that's true. But Linda made it clear that she wanted nothing to do with raising our daughter, and I would never leave Rose without a loving parent to care for her."

"Daddy?" Four-year-old Rose stood at the top of the stairs, staring down through the metal slats in the banister. She hid something behind her back.

Mr. Reed smiled at her. "Yes, baby?"

"I did something bad," Rose said.

"What was it, sweetheart?"

"I tookted the poster pieces."

Mr. Reed climbed the stairs toward her. "What do you mean, you took the pieces?"

"We were in your classroom and they looked so pretty. I wanted to make you something pretty, Daddy."

As Mr. Reed kneeled in front of his daughter, she held up a sheet of pink craft paper for him to see. It was adorned with hand-drawn stick figures of a father and daughter holding hands. And right in the middle of the paper was a note made of the missing poster letters. It read "I LovE yOu dADdy." The big green L was prominently featured as the first letter in the word *LovE*.

Mr. Reed stared at the letter for what seemed like three lifetimes before he wrapped his arms around his daughter. Madison turned to Stuart, ashamed. "I think we made a huge mistake."

Stuart nodded in agreement. "We should go." They slowly backed out the door and quietly shut it. As the door clicked, Mr. Reed still clutched his daughter tightly in his arms.

***

Stuart turned away from the house and walked across the lawn. "I won't lie; I feel kind of bad. Kind of *really* bad."

"I concur; all the evidence seemed to coincide with our assessment," Timothy said.

"I think we should give up, guys," Madison said.

"Everything we do just keeps blowing up in our faces."

As they stepped onto the sidewalk in front of the house, they heard a loud, gruff cough from behind them. They turned to see Stuart's father step out from the shadows. "I knew if I just waited long enough, the three of you would make an appearance."

"Well, you're a detective," Stuart said. "I guess that's your job."

Josiah nodded. "You're right. And you are children. I thought it was you who put that evidence on my desk, and it was too tempting a lead not to follow up on. Now, I have egg on my face."

"I'm sorry, Dad," Stuart said.

"Yeah," Timothy said. "We're really sorry, Mr. Greenbaum."

"Sorry? You know what I have to do to get a warrant? Do you know how much crow I'm going to have to eat? Do you have any idea the size of the crap storm that's going to rain down on me? No. I think we're a little past sorry, kiddos. Come on. Let's get you back home before I slap the cuffs on all of you hooligans."

Josiah nudged them toward his car. "I should haul you all downtown. Luckily for you I'm off-duty."

***

Timothy, Stuart, and Madison rode in the backseat of the

police car. Stuart sat behind his father, his sagging head propped up by the cold window. He stared out into the night, wondering where he had gone wrong.

As the car passed Mr. Alberts's office, a light bulb went off in Stuart's head. He turned, beckoning Timothy and Madison to lean closer to him. "I know who did it. For real this time."

"I think we're in enough trouble as it is," Madison said.

"If you don't want to find your father, that's fine," Stuart said. "But, everything we've done has led us to this moment. If you trust me one more time, I swear you'll be with your dad before the night is over. What do you say?"

Josiah glanced into his rear view mirror as he drove. "What are you three scheming about back there?"

Stuart straightened up. "Nothing. Timothy's not feeling well. He gets car sick. Can you slow down a bit?"

Josiah grumbled as he eased off the accelerator. The car slowed to a crawl and Stuart turned back to Madison. "Well?"

"All right, I'm in," Madison said.

"How about you, Tim?"

"Well, I have been feeling a bit queasy," Timothy said.

"About the case, moron."

"Right. Well, I'm in. But how are we going to escape? These police cars don't allow you to open the back seat."

"After my dad locked himself in here a few years ago, he

built in a fail-safe. Just get ready to run."

Stuart reached under his father's seat and grabbed on to a door-release lever. He pulled it, and the back doors popped up. He slammed his shoulder against the door and it opened. The added wind resistance forced the car to swerve across the road.

Josiah spun the wheel hard as he tried to regain control of the car. "What are you doing, Stuart?"

"Sorry, Dad. We have a case to solve." Stuart jumped out of the car and rolled to a stop, standing as the car screeched to a stop. His father jumped out and ran toward him. Timothy and Madison jumped out of the back seat, without being seen, and ran into the night.

Stuart darted through the yard of a nearby house, jumped the fence, and disappeared into the backyard.

Chapter 17

Final Showdown

Lou Lou Belle's house was as close to being a trailer as one could get without lifting it onto wheels. Painted with nothing but a layer of primer, the home was the antithesis of her chipper personality. In fact, it was easy to see why she spent the majority of her time at the office; living in the squalor of her disgusting hovel for one second longer than needed could make somebody descend into madness, or die of tetanus.

Outside her home sat a collection of rusted debris, which was scattered around the property. The only other structure within half a mile was a small, rotted wooden shed. Several electrical wires ran into the shed from the main house.

"I refuse to believe Lou Lou Belle would be the one you're after," Madison said. "She loved my dad and she wouldn't hurt a fly."

Stuart stood on his tiptoes and peered into a window. He saw Lou Lou Belle thoroughly distracted as she watched TV and ate her microwave dinner. "Really? Because this looks exactly like the type of house a crazed psychopath would grow up in."

Stuart, attempting to find an access point into the house, tripped over an orange extension cord. He picked it up and wriggled it; it wriggled all the way to the shed.

He followed the cord. "This way," he said.

"I just don't see the motive," Madison said.

"Actually, it's really simple," Stuart said. "Lou Lou Belle found out that your father was going to dissolve the company. She loved it too much to let it die."

Stuart reached the shed and grabbed the combination padlock that bolted the door shut. "It can never be easy, can it?"

"Wait right here," Timothy said. He ran off into the night.

"Hey, where are you going?" Stuart said.

"I still don't understand something," Madison said. "How would she ever be able to pull this off?"

"Well, it was difficult. That's for sure. After she found out that your father wanted to dissolve the partnership, she pleaded with him to reconsider. When he wouldn't listen, she snapped. She loved your dad and Mr. Mitchell too much to let them destroy everything. I mean let's face it. She obviously doesn't have much else to live for. She helped build that firm. You said it yourself, Madison: she's been with them since they opened shop."

"But why would she kidnap my father and attack Mr. Mitchell?"

"Escalation. She must've gone over to your house that night to reason with your dad one more time. When he rebuffed her a second time, she felt that she had no other choice but to bring him here."

"What about Mr. Mitchell?" Madison asked.

"When she told Mr. Mitchell that she knew about the dissolution of the partnership, she expected him to be on her side. Unfortunately, he'd decided to go through with the breakup, which left Lou Lou devastated. When Timothy and I visited your father's office, we told her that we thought your dad's partner was a suspect. She had to hurry and carry out her plan—before we contacted Mr. Mitchell and ruled him out as a suspect."

"What was her plan?"

"A détente between Mr. Mitchell and your father so they could work out their problems. Unfortunately, Mr. Mitchell didn't go willingly, and she was forced to drug him just like your father. Too bad she got spooked before she was able to make off with him. I suspect she's going to try again once the police guard is lifted and she can visit him again."

"So this was all done out of love?"

"Kind of. It's sort of sweet, isn't it?"

Madison rolled her eyes. Stuart recanted. "All right. It's nuts. Where is Timothy?"

Timothy emerged from the darkness with an old, rusted tire iron. "Right here. It took me a moment to find the proper material. If you'll excuse me, I'll open this lock now."

Stuart moved out of the way. "Be my guest."

Timothy jammed the iron through the lock loop. "You see, it's all about force. The tire iron acts as a fulcrum. When pressed tight enough against the lock and smashed with enough force, it will cause the lock to snap like a twig."

"What are you going to hit it with?" Madison said.

Timothy reached down and grabbed a large rock from the ground. He reared back and slammed it into the tire iron. The lock snapped in half and fell to the ground, but the sound of the impact echoed for miles around.

Stuart grabbed onto the heavy door. "Great job, genius. You just alerted the whole area."

"You should show me some respect," Timothy said. "I did successfully dismantle this lock."

Stuart grunted as he heaved open the door. "I suppose you did. Now all we have to do is not get caught by the crazy kidnapper!"

Once open, Madison ran forward and flipped the light. She looked inside and tears filled her eyes.

***

"DAD!" Madison saw that her father, while tied to a metal chair, was very much alive. She ran to him, wrapping her arms around his dislocated shoulder and hugging him tight.

"MADISON! My God, it's so good to see you. How did you find me?" Though his smile revealed blood-soaked teeth, and he could barely open his welted, beaten eyes, his delight was obvious. He tried to hug her back. But the rope wrapped around him prevented it.

"Nice to meet you, sir," Stuart said after a few seconds. "Let me get you out of those ropes so you can properly hug your daughter."

Stuart grabbed a hunting knife from the counter and kneeled behind Madison's father. He sliced through the rope, and Mr. Alberts sprung free, grasping his daughter tight.

Timothy cleared his throat, embarrassed to ruin the moment. "I apologize to be a bother, but it would be best if we escaped before the psychopath returned."

Mr. Alberts squeezed his daughter one more time before

releasing her. "You're right. She promised to finish the job once her stories were over." He tried to stand, but his atrophied limbs collapsed underneath him.

Stuart caught him under his left arm before he fell to the floor. "Madison, grab his other arm. Timothy, make sure the coast is clear."

Timothy peeked out into the night. "The coast is not clear."

As Madison positioned herself under her father's arm, Lou Lou Belle threw Timothy down, sauntering into the shed and brandishing a butcher knife. The smile that had been so prevalent on her face was now replaced with a grotesque scowl. "Well, well, well. I thought the cavalry would be a little bigger, maybe with a gun or two."

"We're not scared of you," Madison shouted defiantly.

Timothy disagreed fervently. "Yes we are, Madison. She has a knife."

"She's a coward," Madison said. "Drugging and kidnapping people."

Lou Lou Belle held out her knife toward Madison's heart. "Do you know what I've done to keep that firm afloat? How many phone calls I've answered and arguments I've settled? I've done everything for them! And it was all worth it, because I was in it for something bigger than myself. I thought we were a family. But we weren't a family; families don't break up. Now look at me. Ten years of my life down the drain—all because these two couldn't work out their problems. They were going to take everything from me!"

Mr. Alberts looked up. "I'm sorry you feel that way, but partnerships do dissolve. It doesn't mean you weren't important, or we still didn't love you."

"Love. What do you know about love?"

Stuart struggled to hold Madison's father upright. "How about you don't argue with the crazy lady holding a knife?"

"Good idea. What do you want, Belle?"

"It's too late for that," she said. "You've ruined everything. Now, it's time for you to die. If Peter can't have you, then nobody can."

Belle threw Madison out of the way and lunged. But before Lou Lou Belle could plunge the dagger into Madison's father, Josiah ran through the door. "FREEZE, Belle. Drop the knife and put your hands over your head."

Belle knew she had been licked. She dropped her knife and raised her arms to the ceiling. "I just wanted to help," she said.

***

Stuart leaned against the shed door next to his father. They watched Lou Lou Belle lower her head into the back of a squad car.

"I was doing it out of LOVE! LOVE!" she shouted as an officer closed the door behind her.

"I must say, I'm mighty impressed," Josiah said.

"Me," Stuart said. "What about you? Coming through in the clutch. How'd you do it?"

"Oh, that's an old trade secret. Let's just say we have some lab techs of our own. May not be as good as Timothy's lab, but they'll do in a pinch. They analyzed the ransom note and found two sets of prints. Yours and Lou Lou Belle's. After that it was easy. How about you? You didn't have much time to stop by the tree house after you rolled out of my car."

"I remembered something while you were driving us home. Magazines. Madison said she gave all of her old magazines to Lou Lou Belle once she had turned in her monthly poster project. They were all cut up, so I didn't think anything of it at the time."

Josiah rubbed his son's head. "Well, I'm quite impressed. Maybe you aren't such a degenerate after all. I think your friend's pretty impressed as well." He pointed to an ambulance where a paramedic was examining Madison's father. She sat next to him, grasping his arm so tight she could have cut off his circulation. She waved at Stuart before she turned her attention back to her father.

"I think you earned this son," Josiah said. He took his

fedora off, placing it on Stuart's head. "You're a regular Dan Dash."

The massive fedora slid down his head and covered his eyes. "Does that mean I'm not in trouble?" Stuart asked.

"Are you kidding me? You are grounded for your foreseeable life, my friend."

"But you're not going to shut down Gumshoes, are you?"

Josiah looked over at Timothy, who was carefully studying the crime scene investigators as they gathered evidence.

"You can't pick up that knife with your bare hands!" Timothy shouted. "What kind of case are you trying to build? A terrible one?"

Timothy pulled out a rubber glove from his cargo pants. He lifted up the knife into a plastic evidence bag and sealed it. "See. Just like this. Now you're not contaminating evidence."

Josiah smiled. "I guess it's not the worst thing in the world to have a hobby, but you have to promise me you won't take on any more big cases."

Stuart crossed his fingers behind his back. "I promise."

"That's my boy. Now, let's get you home before your mother chops my head off."

Stuart walked with his father toward the car. Today, he thought, I won't take another big case. But tomorrow is another day.

***

Later that night, Madison ripped down the police tape and opened the door to her home. "It's good to be home."

She ran back outside and walked her father into the house. "I'll bet you'll never get a better night's sleep."

Madison guided her father up the stairs and into his bedroom. She laid him on the bed. "Good night, Dad."

Madison covered her father with a blanket and sat down at the edge of the bed, watching him sleep. A single tear rolled down her face. It was not long before more followed; soon, a flood of tears streamed down her face.

These were not the tears she had become accustomed to shedding recently. No, these were tears of joy; utter and complete joy. She lay down next to her father and drifted off to sleep.

Epilogue

The following week Stuart and Timothy walked down a hallway at school. They looked at a gaggle of popular girls, but found Madison nowhere in sight. The girls ignored them as they passed.

"I guess everything's back to normal, ay Tim?" Stuart said.

"Perhaps it's for the best," Timothy said. "We might've flown too close to the sun, assuming that we could not be picked on."

"Yeah. It's a shame, though. I really thought this would change things."

"Well, this will be Madison's first day back at school. Perhaps if she treats us kindly, we'll be back in their good graces."

"Why wouldn't I treat you kindly?" Madison said from

behind them. "You saved my dad's life."

Stuart and Timothy turned. Madison greeted them with a warm, endearing group hug. She squeezed them so hard that Timothy could not breathe. He slapped Madison on the back. "Too hard."

Madison released them. "Sorry. I'm just so excited things are back to normal."

Stuart's eyes dropped. "Yeah. Back to normal. So, I guess you'll be back to the popular crowd. I'll see you around."

Madison lifted Stuart's head until their eyes met. "No way. Did you know not one of them came over to see my dad the whole week I was home? I told them all to shove off."

Stuart smiled. "Really?"

Madison nudged between Timothy and Stuart, and latched her arms through theirs. "Yup. So what are we going to do tonight?"

"We could see a mov——"

Timothy's thought was interrupted by a short, freckled sixth-grader named Oliver. "Are you the Gumshoes?"

Stuart, Madison, and Timothy responded in unison. "You bet."

"You've got to help me," Oliver said. "They say I took money from the dance fund, but I didn't do it. Can you help me? Will you take the case?"

Stuart, Timothy, and Madison did not have to think for more than a few seconds before they looked down at Oliver and nodded. "You bet we will."

Oliver jumped up and down with glee. "Oh thank you, thank you, thank you."

As they basked in the glow of their newfound friendship, a massive figure blocked the light at the end of the hall. Chet and his cronies ambled toward them.

"NERDS!" he screamed. "I heard Madison's no longer the 'it' girl. Y'all have no protection. You are so dead!"

"Uh oh," Stuart said. "We should run." With that, the Gumshoes and Oliver took off down the hall with Chet and his cronies close on their heels.

www.ingramcontent.com/pod-product-compliance
Lightning Source LLC
Chambersburg PA
CBHW070951180726
48291CB00004B/1237